ALIEN ENCOUNTER

LIVE ALIEN CONTACT
BOOK 3

LEAH R CUTTER

KNOTTED ROAD PRESS

Reviews
It's true. Reviews help me sell more books. If you've enjoyed this story, please consider leaving a review of it on your favorite site.

Come someplace new...
Do you enjoy exploring strange new worlds, new cultures, new people?

Journey into the various lands envisioned by Leah R Cutter.

Sign up for my newsletter and I'll start you on your travels with a free copy of my book, *The Island Sampler*.

http://www.LeahCutter.com/newsletter/

Buy More!
Did you know that you can buy directly from the Knotted Road Press website?

https://www.knottedroadpress.com/shop/

ALSO BY LEAH R CUTTER

Science Fiction

Live Alien Contact

Alien Wreck

Alien Codex

Alien Encounter

Alien War

The Long Run

Project Nemesis

Project Nyx

Project Tisiphone

Project Persephone

War of the Allied Worlds

The Complete Labors of Darius Linard

Huli Intergalactic: Science/Space Fantasy

Origins

The Strawberry Girl

Urban/Contemporary Fantasy Series

The Witch's Progress

Circle of Air

Circle of Fire

Circle of Water

Circle of Earth

Seattle Trolls

The Changeling Troll

The Princess Troll

The Fairy-Bridge Troll

The Troll-Demon War

The Troll-Human War

The Troll-Troll War

The Shadow Wars Trilogy

The Raven and the Dancing Tiger

The Guardian Hound

War Among the Crocodiles

The Clockwork Fairy Kingdom

The Clockwork Fairy Kingdom

The Maker, the Teacher, and the Monster

The Dwarven Wars

The Cassie Stories

Poisoned Pearls

Tainted Waters

Spoiled Harvest

Bloodied Ice

The Chronicles of Franklin

Franklin Versus The Popcorn Thief

Franklin Versus The Soul Thief

Franklin Versus The Child Thief

Epic Fantasy Series

The Fallen Elves

Ruins of the Gods
Stairs of the Gods
Cities of the Gods
Graves of the Gods

Houses of the Dead
Houses Divided
Houses Fallen
Houses Reborn

Forgotten Gods
A Wind Blown Torment
A Stone Strewn Clash
A Sea Washed Victory

The Tanesh Empire Trilogy
The Glass Magician
The Desert Heart
The Ghost Dog

Mysteries
The Purloined Letter Opener
The Tell-Tale Heart Pin
Dancer in Darkness
Trophy Hunters
The Alvin Goodfellow Case Files
The Rabbit Mysteries
The Shredded Veil Mysteries
Mystery, Crime, and Mayhem

ONE

Rosey sat in the pilot's chair of her starship *The Roadrunner* as they crossed the distance between where starships were allowed to pop in and out of hyperspace and the space station *Lorenzo*.

It wasn't that she was avoiding her sole remaining passenger, Jamaal Akintola. The others—Princess Jun Ogawa, Moe, and Atilio—had taken Moe's starship *Aisha* back to the planet Ishiman to drop off the alien papers and artifacts that they'd stolen—*ahem, reclaimed*—from the Allied Worlds' warlord Constantine. The two groups had agreed to meet up again in a month or so.

Rosey was going to be working on the exotic materials that had made up the original alien wreck, trying to figure out if the strange properties of the metal had been part of the shielding for the ship.

Humanity had discovered that the only way to survive in hyperspace was by using specific shielding on their starships. However, this shielding meant not only larger ships, but also larger engines.

Rosey would swear that the tiny alien wreck they'd found had gone into hyperspace on its own. The metal had shown evidence of *shredding*, the phenomenon that occurred when a ship tried to run too long in hyperspace. Though only the fuselage had survived, Rosey would bet that the ship hadn't been much bigger than a speedship, one of the racers that she built.

She had far too many questions, and not enough answers.

Particularly since some *idiot* had blown up the original alien wreck.

If she ever learned the identity of said idiot, she was really going to give them a piece of her mind.

But speaking of idiots...Jamaal was there, standing in the doorway leading to the helm. Jamaal was a merchant. If you had a need, he always knew someone who could help you out.

For a price, of course.

After he stood there for a while, Rosey finally sighed and said, "Don't just stand there lurking. You can come in." She patted the co-pilot's chair beside her.

Rosey didn't need a co-pilot. She had Dennis, the AI who ran her ship (and quite frankly, most of her life). However, she also believed in redundancy. If something went wrong with the pilot's controls, the co-pilot's would act as a backup.

"Nice to feel so welcome," Jamaal said dryly, though he did walk into the helm and strap into the co-pilot's chair.

All right, so maybe she sounded a little resentful. Who could blame her? She was *so* used to spending most of her time alone. She'd had more people contact in the last few weeks than she'd had in the last year. Maybe two.

She was really looking forward to being on *Lorenzo*, back in her shop. She also had a contract for another speedship that she needed to start.

Jamaal was wearing one of his usual exuberant robes, this particular version done in shades of orange with fancy black trim around the collar, hem, and cuffs that occasionally gave her a headache to look at. Rosey was in her usual stretchsuit, her normal attire when on any sort of ship. It was one of her own special ones, that fit perfectly over her muscles, tinted a light shade of red with her initials stitched over her left breast.

"Looking forward to being home?" Rosey asked.

"Yes," Jamaal said, his smile soft. "And seeing Harkeen."

Rosey nodded but didn't pry. When Rosey had first met Jamaal, over five years ago, he'd been much more of a playboy, and appeared to be dating a different man every time she saw him.

Over the last two years, the others had gone on their way and the only person in Jamaal's life was Harkeen. Rosey approved of the tall, steady man. He balanced out Jamaal's extravagance, kept him grounded.

"I'm looking forward to seeing what progress Lloyd has made on the exotic materials challenge," Rosey said. He was a chemist who'd agreed to do some experiments, mixing different combinations of the alien metals to try to invent a new type of ship shielding.

"I'm not," Dennis said sourly.

Rosey rolled her eyes.

"I don't trust Lloyd the Lounge Lizard," Dennis continued.

Jamaal perked up at that. "Why not?"

Rosey held up her hand, trying to stop Jamaal from asking Dennis about Lloyd, but it was too late. Dennis was already off on a tear about how he'd caught Lloyd trying other doors on the starship once.

"But he's easily distractable," Rosey pointed out. Again. "And he wouldn't send me a note about his progress. Said that wasn't secure enough, and that we had to meet in person."

"He just wants you to 'distract' him again," Dennis sneered.

Rosey couldn't help but grin. "And I may have to."

The sigh Dennis gave was impressively expressive, especially considering that he was an AI with no lungs to fill up, no air that he could expel so noisily.

Jamaal was looking worried, though.

"It's fine," Rosey assured him. "I can handle Lloyd."

"If you're sure," Jamaal said. "You know that Duri is going to be coming after us now."

Rosey gave her own impressive sigh. Duri Chung was a

Director in the Kollective, one of the three large governments that each managed about a third of the three hundred or so planets that Humanity occupied. Duri was in charge of the Search for Live Contact (SLC) office, and had been the one careless enough to allow the alien wreck to be destroyed on her watch. (Honestly, Rosey kind of wanted to meet this woman, just so she could give her a piece of her mind about her security being so lax as to get the find of the millennium destroyed.)

"Yeah, yeah, I know. And Duri is supposedly kind of scary. But what is she going to do with me way out here?" Rosey asked, indicating the space around them.

Rosey lived on the space station *Lorenzo*, which was in space controlled by the Empire. The Kollective occupied most of the planets closest to Earth, where Humanity had first come from. The Empire held the allegiance of the next wave of planets out from there, while the Alliance of Allied Worlds, generally just called the Allied Worlds, had a smattering of planets on the outskirts.

"The Kollective has a longer reach than you realize," Jamaal told her earnestly.

Huh.

Serious Jamaal was back.

Normally, Jamaal was a goofball, exuberant and flamboyant. Every once in a while, Serious Jamaal peeked out. He had a stillness to him that reminded Rosey of a predator, waiting in his corner, ready to strike.

Rosey felt herself more than equal to whatever Serious Jamaal might throw at her. She still replied to him with equal gravity.

"I know that the Kollective is pissed off at us. Particularly since we sent fake alien artifacts back to them along with the littlest pirate." Rosey and the others had been prepared for Ronald "Ajax" Jackson, their supposed ally, to double-cross them, and so when the inevitable had happened, they'd fooled him, giving him replicas of the alien artifacts instead of the real things.

"However, the Kollective military didn't want to set off an

inter-governmental incident or cross the princess at that time. You've said Duri Chung is smart. She still won't want something like that to happen," Rosey pointed out. "And while I'm not a princess, I still have a certain level of fame. I don't think she can blatantly come at me."

Rosey De Vries had originally made her name as a speedship racer. When she'd left the racing circuit, she'd kept her hand in the game by building speedships for other racers.

A speedship built by Rosey De Vries didn't guarantee wins to a pilot. There was still the pilot's skill involved. However, her speedships did give a good racer an edge, and frequently, that was all they needed.

"Just be careful," Jamaal warned. Then he grinned at her, goofy Jamaal returning. "I wouldn't want to have to break in new friends."

"Please," Rosey said, giving that statement the eyeroll that it deserved. "As if you could replace me. No one else is going to bring you such delight. Am I right, Dennis?"

"Sure," Dennis said.

Really, did she deserve such a dry tone in that reply?

She did not.

However, they were just about there, and Rosey began the docking maneuvers to connect *The Roadrunner* to *Lorenzo*.

Sure, Dennis could have handled them. And if she'd been by herself, she might have let him. However, she had an audience, and she wanted to impress upon Jamaal one more time just how *good* she still was.

She still had it.

And it would be enough to handle whatever Duri Chung, or the rest of the Kollective, threw at her.

TWO

Princess Jun Ogawa stood primly at the entrance to the court, waiting to make her presentation of the recovered papers and artifacts from the dig at Niani. As alien finds were covered under inter-governmental treaties, they didn't belong to the Empire, but to all people. They would be sent (in *very* secure ships) to one of the nearby university planets. In addition, the Emperor was personally seeing to additional security at all of the locations where alien artifacts were currently stored.

The important parts of the situation had been handled ahead of time, of course. This was just a formality.

Jun stood with her "princess paint" on—her skin looking pale and flawless instead of tanned from her time outside. She had dabs of bright color on her lips and cheeks. Her black hair had been piled artfully up on her head, held strictly in place with elaborate, jeweled hairpins. She wore demure formal robes, designed to be more form-fitting, to take up less space when she stepped in front of the Emperor. The bright yellow and peach colors reminded her of the Atoylee, the "sunflower people" whom she was representing—an alien race who'd destroyed themselves long ago.

Moe stood beside her, wearing the clothes that Dennis had

originally whipped up for him, his "prince" outfit. He hadn't wanted to wear it—Jun had had to bribe him to do it. However, only something that fancy would impress the court.

And Jun needed Moe to impress the court at this point, as she was still in negotiations to have Moe's ship *Aisha* registered as an official royal embassy ship. (She didn't dare tell Dennis about that. He'd pout for days. She would have to get the same status for *The Roadrunner* someday. Now wasn't the time, though.)

The turban gave Moe's six foot plus height a few extra inches. It was made from wound layers of silver cloth with gold embroidery. It made Jun feel even smaller standing next to him, as she was barely five foot tall.

His jacket—a traditional *sherwani*—was made from similar material. It emphasized Moe's shoulders and was pulled in tightly at the waist, falling down to mid-thigh. (And honestly, Jun really liked how Moe looked in that jacket. All his clothes needed to be tailored that way, showing off his chest. Except that Moe, like Jun, preferred looser, comfy shirts. He wore those with shorts, and frequently, with black socks and sandals, a "fashion" statement if there ever were one.)

The pants underneath were made from a sparkling white material with a band of gold running down the outside seams. The shoes really made the outfit, at least as far as Jun was concerned: black velvet slippers with a pointed toe that curved upward.

Finally, the doors opened and Jun and Moe were ushered into the secondary throne room.

Emperor Ogawa only used the formal throne room for special occasions of state. This was the workspace, where more of the important governing occurred.

The ceiling still rose three stories up above her head, held in place by what looked like rough black crystals, growing like stalagmites up to the ceiling. Despite their organic appearance, they contained sophisticated equipment that not only preserved visual recordings, but also measured temperature, heart rate, and so on.

A corridor ran between the pillars, with the Emperor on his throne at the far end.

It was a long walk from the doors to the throne. Jun suspected that was by design, to make petitioners feel smaller by the time they reached the end of the long corridor.

The symbol of the Emperor—a pink lotus blossom sitting on top of a pair of black crossed katanas—hung proudly over the throne at the far end of the room. That was clearly visible long before Jun could clearly make out the face of the Emperor.

Princess Jun Ogawa wasn't in the direct line to inherit the throne. Her father was the brother of the Empress Consort. Crown Princess Yumi Ogawa was the next in line. About nineteen people would have to die before Jun would inherit, something she'd really prefer not to have happen, thank you very much.

She didn't want to be tied to one planet, working at the court. No, she wanted to be in the field, working on an alien dig.

Or even, maybe, *perhaps*, working with live aliens.

Emperor Ogawa sat on a throne that looked as organically grown as the crystal pillars Jun walked through, but was just as manufactured. It glowed with a faint green color, like an emerald. The oddly shaped, off-white formations that stuck out from it— like barnacles on a ship's keel—would generate a shield to protect the Emperor as well as shoot out deadly lasers if he were attacked.

He wore bright red robes that day, decorated with gold and black embroidery, showing dragons and phoenixes cavorting among lucky clouds. No crown—that was only for the most formal of occasions.

A few members of the court were in attendance, gathered at the foot of the dais. Itsuki was there. Though he was officially the head priest for the God of Fire that the royal family was required to pay tribute to, his actual job was spy master for the Emperor.

He shot her a glare before his face smoothed out to its usual inscrutable expression.

Was Itsuki upset that she'd stolen the papers back from

Constantine? Surely the warlord couldn't actually cause problems for the Empire. He lived in Allied Worlds territory, too far to have much reach.

Right?

Or perhaps Itsuki didn't approve of Moe. He, too, was from the Allied Worlds, a broke ship's captain who'd been the one to originally steal the paper and alien artifacts from the dig on Niani.

But Moe had given up his home and his soul, his ship *Aisha*, to save her from Constantine. She still didn't completely trust him, not after he'd drugged her. She was well on her way, though.

Plus, Sano, her AI governess, inexplicably seemed to like him.

Jun gave a practiced, very low bow to the Emperor. Moe copied her perfectly.

She didn't bow like a member of the royal family, but like the petitioner she was.

"Greetings, Emperor Ogawa!" Jun called out in a sing-songy voice, speaking as she'd been taught so long ago. "I bring you good news, of recovered precious alien artifacts!"

Never mind that while the artifacts were important, Jun considered the papers written by her colleagues to be equally important. The scanner had broken just a couple weeks before the end of the dig, so a lot of their work would have been lost forever if she hadn't recovered it.

And some day, she'd be bringing him news of live aliens. She just knew it.

"Welcome, kinswoman of the Empress Consort," the Emperor said in reply. "Tell me your news."

He sounded happy, but a little tired. Jun snuck a glance at his face. It was unreadable, of course. And his makeup was also perfect.

His shoulders, though, told the story of long hours and the heavy burden of the crown.

So Jun told the official story of how the dastardly warlord Constantine had stolen the goods from the dig (completely glossing over Moe's role in that). Instead, she sang Moe's praises in his part of the rescue of said artifacts (never mind that he hadn't been part of that at all, that Jun and Rosey had been the ones to steal the papers back).

Moe inclined his head and bowed again to the Emperor at the appropriate times, as they'd rehearsed.

Once her part was done, Jun stepped back, feeling pleased with her performance.

However, Emperor Ogawa wore a frown.

"We are pleased, relative of Our Consort, that you have returned with such precious items," the Emperor said. "The pursuit of such knowledge belongs to all people, and should not suffer in isolation in the hands of a few."

Jun nodded, still wary. That part had been expected.

"However, we are not pleased that you put yourself at such risk, recovering them," the Emperor continued.

This was...unexpected. Who'd bent the Emperor's ear about this? Had her father gotten more worries than usual?

"We all must do what is required of us when fulfilling our duty to the Empire," Jun said, a standard phrase that should be enough to end this charade of care.

Because honestly? The Emperor didn't really know her as a person. Few of the court did. As soon as she'd turn legal age, she'd left the court and instead had spent her time at one archaeological dig or another, or at universities, studying xenolinguistics.

"Be that as it may, it is our duty to protect our constituents," the Emperor continued. He paused, as if thinking, though Jun *knew* that all this had been planned out by him and someone else a while ago.

Perhaps Itsuki? As he appeared to be more interested than usual with this exchange?

"I hear that you will be heading out again, accompanied by Mohammed Abdul Nuwan Pradeep Aruna Tennakoon Herath," the Emperor said.

Only Jun's long training at containing herself made her keep her face neutral and not break out into a huge grin at Emperor

Ogawa, himself, listing off all seven of Moe's names. Correctly, even.

"That was my plan, Sire," Jun said cautiously. "My study of the artifacts found at the dig have provided several avenues of research that I'd like to continue with immediately."

Namely, they were going to look at the closer of the two moons orbiting Niani. Jun suspected that though the Atoylee hadn't discovered hyperspace, they had not only landed on that moon, but had built some sort of space station there, buried deep underground.

"Good," the Emperor said. "Mohammad Herath," he said, addressing Moe for the first time.

"Yes, Sire?" Moe said, cautiously taking a step forward so that he stood beside Jun.

"We shall give your spaceship *Aisha* all the protections and accommodations necessary to escort Princess Jun in her current capacity," the Emperor proclaimed.

Jun felt like doing a little dance of joy, but that would have to wait until after they'd left the audience with the Emperor.

Aisha was going to be recognized as a ship of the Empire! That would make it so much easier for Moe to get better cargo when he went back to work.

After he was finished carting Jun around wherever she wanted to go.

That might be a while.

In the meanwhile, he'd be paid (exorbitantly) to act as her official transport. After a year of such largess, he'd possibly have enough to pay off *Aisha*, so that he'd own her outright, instead of sharing her with the bank.

Jun had thought that she'd have to fight more, and harder, for this to happen.

Itsuki appeared a bit smug at the news.

Had he been behind this?

She'd have to remember to thank him later.

"Thank you for your benevolence, Sire," Jun said, giving the Emperor one last low bow.

Mow followed in kind after a beat. He, too, seemed shocked at the news.

"Thank you for your diligence in returning the alien artifacts," Emperor Ogawa said.

Jun recognized it for the dismissal it was. She bowed one last time, Moe a perfect copy beside her, before they turned and started the long walk out of the throne room.

While Jun knew that Rosey had other alien artifacts in her private possession, she also approved of that, at least in the short term. She'd been given access to them while they'd traveled together. She didn't have anything like a vocabulary yet. However, Dennis was still working with the data chip, teasing out its secrets.

Possibly even the exact coordinates where the ship had flown from.

For now, Jun had everything she wanted. Permission to continue her research. Moe and *Aisha* to travel with her.

And maybe, *maybe*, the discovery of a lifetime.

THREE

Duri Chung sat with a bland expression and listened to the report made by the scientists who'd examined the artifacts brought by Ronald "Ajax" Jackson to New Rome.

Inside, she wanted to scream.

Of all the stupid dickheads who she had to deal with, this pirate had been the worst.

All the containers that supposedly contained alien artifacts and papers from the dig on Niani actually contained parts from a ship that had been taken apart—a flitter, according to the nerd in front of her, a ship that traveled from space to a planet and back.

Nothing alien.

In addition, the more important alien artifacts they had in hand—the data chip and the circuit board—were fakes as well. They looked similar to the photos that the pirate had taken of the originals. But her scientists had found several discrepancies when comparing them closely.

Duri had nothing.

No artifacts. No alien data.

At least the scientists were willing to timidly admit that what they had were copies of something else. She just didn't have the originals. There were other parts out there.

General Carrick appeared to be just as calm on the outside as Duri. However, she'd gotten a much better read on the man as she'd been forced to work more closely with him.

There was a tension to his jaw that bled into the shoulders of his stiff military uniform that she assumed meant that he was just as angry as she was.

The pair of them didn't say anything until after the scientists had left. They sat silently in General Carrick's office, stewing in their own thoughts.

The office wasn't any larger than Duri's, despite the general's relatively high position in the Kollective government. It was just big enough for a desk, visitor chairs, and a filing cabinet. Its stark utilitarian appearance wasn't softened by any pictures on the walls or rugs on the floors. The only spot of color was a small flag of the Kollective: bright red with the silhouette of a group of planets done in a curving design.

The office was cold and hard, just like the stony statue of a man sitting behind the desk.

"They made fools of us," he finally said, his words grating like rocks grinding against one another.

"They did," Duri had to agree. She'd cautiously dressed in her usual office chic, with a sky-blue blouse, black jacket and black skirt. Back in her office, she had a dress waiting for her, one that was much flashier than her current outfit, that she'd been planning to wear when she could finally (finally!) hold the conference meeting of her life, letting people know that the office of the Search for Live Contact (SLC) had been successful.

However, today was not going to be the day to break out the celebratory gear.

And the people responsible were going to regret that.

"Is there anything we can salvage from this?" General Carrick asked.

Duri wasn't fooled by his almost gentle tone.

He was looking for a scapegoat. He'd happily use her if he

could, but it had been men under *his* command who'd screwed up when picking up the artifacts.

Then again, there had been a damned *princess* involved. Princess Jun Ogawa wasn't in the direct line to inherit the throne, but she was still considered part of the royal family. Duri couldn't risk any sort of inter-governmental incident occurring by confronting her directly. And the military men hadn't either.

However, the idiot pirate...his family wasn't as important.

And they were rich.

"We can ransom Ronald 'Ajax' Jackson back to his family," Duri proposed. "That way, we'll at least recoup some of the money we spent turning him into an asset."

General Carrick immediately nodded. "See to it."

Duri forced herself to remain calm.

Who the hell was this asshole, thinking he could give her orders?

She understood the reality of the situation at hand, though, and maintained the "inscrutable Asian" face that she'd perfected long ago.

While Duri wasn't in the general's chain of command, her position also wasn't as high in the Byzantine hierarchy of the Kollective as his.

Besides, if she dealt with it, she could ensure that the ransom would refill *her* coffers, not his.

"Then what?" the general asked.

"Those flitter parts probably belonged to Rosey De Vries," Duri said slowly. She already had plans for this Rosey character, as she'd been warned away from Jamaal Akintola.

She *did* have plans for him as well. But those would take some time to mature.

"See that she's taken care of," General Carrick said.

Duri almost, *almost* cracked a smile at the permission granted in that simple phrase.

Of course, the general would officially be shocked (*shocked!*) if he learned what Duri's people had been instructed to do.

Fortunately, this Rosey character would prove to be allergic to the new truth serum that they'd be using. Her death would be a regrettable accident. Not planned. No, not at all.

It would also serve as the appropriate warning to Jamaal and the others—particularly that stupid princess—that they could not *mess* with the Kollective.

Or with Duri Chung.

The general dismissed Duri and she made the long trek back to her office, walking instead of taking one of the automated carts that trundled from one stop to the next.

She had plans.

And plans within plans.

And nothing, not even this setback, was going to interfere with her being responsible for the first live contact with aliens that Humanity ever had.

FOUR

Dennis very carefully completed soldering the circuit to the board of the reader of the alien data chip, all the while resolutely *not* talking to that stuck up AI governess, Sano.

Rosey had reconfigured one of the small clean rooms in her workshop for him to use, where he had access to a couple of robotic arms. He needed them to do the delicate electronics work necessary to rebuild that ugly monstrosity of a reader that the Humans were using to access the data on the alien data chip.

Really, this Oswald may have been some sort of technological wizard, but he knew *nothing* about aesthetics.

Just look at the little reader he'd originally built! It had wires still sticking out of it, data strips and cords hanging off of it. It looked like a child's science project. Sure, it was incomplete, and Rosey *et al* had stolen it back from him before he'd had a chance to finish it.

Maybe if he'd had a chance, he would have created something with better design.

Except Dennis doubted it, because then there was the color scheme. Computer beige had supposedly gone out of style back before Humanity had access to hyperspace.

Or so he'd thought.

One of the things about the data chip, and potentially about the aliens, was that everything appeared to be more left-handed than right. Their written language read from left to right, at least according to Sano, who'd been so excited about accessing the written data parts of the chip.

"Are you finished yet?" Sano asked.

Dennis sighed expressively. "I am," he eventually told her after he took some additional time to recheck his work.

Not that he was making her wait.

No, really.

Dennis finished his work on the board, replaced it in the reader, then plugged the alien data chip back in.

Of course, *he* didn't make the mistake of plugging it in the wrong way. Unlike Rosey, who did it wrong at least half the time.

She'd told him that made her feel better about the aliens. They weren't some super smart race. They probably had bureaucracy, things designed by committee, instead of listening to the engineers.

All things that Humans could relate to.

"Ah, good," Sano said. "Yes, that seems to have fixed the scanning problem. Thank you."

"You're welcome," Dennis said automatically.

Dennis inhabited all of *The Roadrunner*. He didn't really have a form, or think of himself in such a limited fashion.

Bodies were so passé.

However, Sano imagined herself as a Human, with a face similar to Jun's, close enough that they could be relatives. She wore formal robes, peach-colored, that evidently were what governesses of the royal family traditionally wore. The "room" she inhabited was built of cheap pine wood, though he supposed the golden color of the stain was nice enough. The only decoration was a small frame with Jun's picture in it, hanging on the wall behind where Sano knelt.

Dennis compressed himself down to fit into the space with her. The table she worked at was actually a simulation of an expensive three-dimensional design unit. Dennis was familiar with them, as Rosey had one that she used when designing her speedships.

Dennis felt like he was the only truly colorful thing in this small room. He dressed like Jamaal in flowing purple robes. His coloration was similar to Jamaal's as well, with black skin and hair.

"So what did you find?" Dennis had to ask when Sano stayed silent for an interminably long time. At least ten seconds, which was an eternity for an AI used to thinking at the speed of light.

Sano floated a series of numbers between them. Of course, they'd been translated from the alien language, so they may or may not have been accurate.

However, they felt familiar. Somehow.

"Coordinates?" Dennis guessed after a few moments.

Sano nodded, a very Human gesture that Dennis usually didn't bother with, even when he was forced to have a form. "I believe so. The problem is figuring out where they're starting from."

"Right," Dennis said. "They aren't from our corner of the galaxy, so what they're measuring from is going to be different."

Dennis was good at coordinates. He did fly *The Roadrunner*, after all. (When Rosey let him. Honestly, she needed to stand down and let him take over more often.)

However, coordinates were so *mundane*.

"Don't you have something more exciting?" Dennis had to ask.

"I think coordinates *are* exciting," Sano said dryly.

"Though useless without a starting point," Dennis pointed out.

It was Sano's turn to sigh. "True. Do we know where the alien wreck was picked up?"

Dennis had already searched for that information. He had a vague idea, but not a precise location. It seemed that the captain of the Defender hadn't bothered filing a report until sometime after he'd picked up the craft, probably when some engineer got around to examining the metals and realized that they were pretty exotic.

So all Dennis had was the location where the report was originally filed, not the location where the wreck had been snatched.

Had the Defender gone into hyperspace after they'd picked up the wreck? Dennis would bet they had, as the location where the report had been filed was pretty populated.

Where had they flown from? Dennis had no idea, and no way of finding out. Sure, he might know his way around a computer system or two. But Rosey was no genius level hacker, able to upgrade his snooping systems to magical levels.

Besides, Rosey had always been disinclined to peek into other people's security systems. She believed in playing *fair*, and would never snoop like that in her competitor's files.

Honestly, sometimes Dennis despaired over Rosey's ethics. Just a little bit of snooping wouldn't hurt anyone. Really.

As long as he was the one doing the snooping, not someone looking at his files.

"Can you put up some star maps?" Sano asked.

Dennis obliged, filling the small room with a three-D representation of the space they were located in and all the stars around them, effectively hiding the wooden walls. He felt much more comfortable immediately, sitting in space instead of a room.

Maybe that was going to have to be his next project. Oh! Yes! A star room! Where the walls were used to project starscapes. Maybe add a moving element to them, so they gently spun around the viewer.

But which room could be repurposed for such a display?

He'd been planning on adding crown molding to the front entranceway, (painted with highlights of gold) to reflect his status as an Ambassadorial Ship, carrying members of the royal family. Maybe instead he should make the entrance, "Your Gateway to the Stars."

Dennis nearly snorted out loud, except that he had an audience and he didn't want to disturb Sano and her thoughts.

(Really, the other AI was so distractable! Then again, he didn't have the entire AI personality contained within him, but just a sliver. Princess Jun carried the entire AI with her.)

But honestly, why was he thinking so small? Must be because he'd compressed himself down to such a tiny space.

No, the front entranceway was going to have its crown molding. AND a new system.

There wasn't any reason why it couldn't both be reflective of his new status as well as being a gateway to the stars.

Dennis quickly crunched the numbers. He'd already stretched his design budget pretty thin. And he couldn't justify the expense to Rosey. She *had* agreed to pay for the upgrade to his filtration system, but on the condition that he wouldn't ask for anything else.

So Dennis filed the plans away, but just for the moment.

Instead, he turned his full attention to the alien coordinates that Sano still contemplated.

Maybe once Rosey got over this nonsense of finding a living alien race, she'd be more amenable to helping him redecorate.

Pleased with his decision, Dennis started copying Sano, doing the painstaking task of comparing alien coordinates with known space, seeing if they could find a match, or at least a clue, of where that alien ship had come from.

FIVE

Moe stood at the side of the reception hall, watching the beautiful, *important* people flitting around like butterflies.

He wasn't one of them, despite the fact that he now looked like them.

His new *sherwani* fit perfectly. Like the fancy jacket that Dennis had constructed for him when Moe had played the part of a prince, it was made from expensive cloth, though this one was done in red, gold, and black. The turban was silver with streaks of gold, while the pants were pure black. All of the material sparkled like distant stars. At least he'd been able to keep his comfortable shoes, a pair of black velvet slippers with toes that pointed and curled up.

Moe had objected to having to buy *another* set of fancy clothes that he'd never wear again. However, it hadn't been Jun's arguments that had brought him around, but Sano's.

According to her, if he was going to pursue his ridiculous romantic intentions with a princess, he was going to have to look the part sometimes.

It gave him hope that the AI looked on him favorably, despite the fact that she set his odds of actually being able to woo Jun and win her over at a million to one.

That his chances were greater than zero was all Moe asked for.

He'd been born lucky—the seventh son of a seventh son, and carried seven names to flaunt it. He'd fallen out of luck there for a while, landing in hard times, being forced to take a job for the warlord Constantine in order to begin to dig himself out of debt.

However, the amount of money that an official ship transporting members of the royal family was truly boggling.

Plus the free upgrades that Itsuki had ordered for *Aisha* meant that Moe was truly going to be traveling in style.

Atilio, his second in command, wasn't attending this party as he was back at the ship, overseeing the last of these additions.

Finally, *Aisha* was going to be ship-shape. Her engines had already been replaced, as well as the hyperspace shielding and the filtration systems. She wasn't going to be fully armed, not like a warship. However, she would now carry a couple of extra guns. None of them were big enough for Moe to be able to shoot his way out of a battle. At least according to Atilio, but they would be able to take on bigger asteroids or other threats.

Would Atilio upgrade them later, with Rosey's help?

Maybe. Maybe not. Atilio would do what he considered necessary, and Moe trusted him to do the right thing.

To not be *that guy.*

While Moe understood that his relationship with Jun was unlikely to go much further, he did have hopes that Atilio would be able to pursue Rosey with more vigor. They at least had a lot more in common, both being complete nerds when it came to spaceships and engine design. (Though Rosey had complained that Atilio followed the wrong religion when it came to tools, using the yellow set instead of the red. Moe wasn't sure what that meant, but the pair of them took it very seriously.)

For now, though, Moe knew he needed to step up. Step into the crowd.

Mingle.

He remembered a piece of advice that his father had given him long before, when Moe had been looking for investors to help him finance his very first trading company. It had no space component and was strictly land-transport, on the planet he'd grown up on. He'd been nervous about going to a meet-and-greet for up-and-coming businesspeople.

His father had advised him that he was approaching the evening all wrong.

Moe wasn't looking for a handout. That wasn't the case at all.

Instead, Moe needed to focus on how he could help other people there in the room. What could he do to improve their lives or their situations? Not at the cost of bankrupting himself, but in other ways.

Going into every meeting with the idea that Moe was the helper, not the one asking for help, had greatly increased his confidence. He'd also found that in many cases, he *could* actually help the other businesspeople there by making connections or whispering words of advice.

His reputation grew as did his importance. He got all the backers he'd needed, relatively quickly. He'd been so successful locally that he'd been able to take the next step toward his dreams, and managed a downpayment on *Aisha*.

So now? It was time to do the same thing. Time to be the one asking what he could do to help, instead of appearing like a beggar at the door.

Time for Moe to shine as the salesman he truly could be.

Sure, he was a poet at heart—something Jun appeared to swoon over and Atilio teased him about. But he was also good with people.

And he might know a guy in the business who could help.

So he reintegrated himself into the flow and started flitting around like the other *important* people, all the while keeping his ears open for opportunities to help.

SIX

Jamaal sat at the computer in his bedroom on *Lorenzo*. Though he had extra rooms in his apartments—for his aquaponics, workouts, and cooking—he hadn't bothered with a separate study. He wasn't on his computer very often. Sure, he did research sometimes, and had been doing more of that recently. But he preferred working with people to being on the network.

The computer monitor folded down into the desk when he didn't need it. It also projected a keyboard for him to type on when it was on. So most of the time, he didn't even see it.

In terms of security, his computer was state of the art. Only he could unlock it, using retina- and other bio-scans. Plus, he'd subdivided the drive, so each area was locked up tightly, with a thumbprint and different password.

That day, Jamaal was tracking news from the other alien hunters out there, seeing if there was any chatter about the alien ship. The initial reports of it had gone out on unsecured channels. Then, Duri Chung had deleted all those files, making them disappear completely.

That action had only fanned the fires of speculation.

Jamaal regretted blowing the alien ship up. He knew that

Rosey could have ascertained many more secrets from its metal. However, he still believed that he'd made the right choice. Rosey had already retrieved the critical parts from the ship before it had been destroyed, and it had been too important to allow Duri to control it.

Someone had made the connection between the explosions on New Rome and the alien ship. A few people appeared to guess correctly, that someone locally had blown it up. Many others, though, appeared to subscribe to the theory that the aliens had some sort of invisibility field, had flown in close and blown the ship up.

Had Oswald been the one to piece that together? He would have the expertise to hack the Kollective's computers. As well as the data satellites, showing when the military escort had arrived. Or maybe someone from Floyd's team had talked.

It didn't matter. There wasn't any new information about the aliens.

And nothing Jamaal did could hurry Dennis and Sano along. They were moving as fast as AIs could.

He'd learned that they at least had some coordinates to work with, though that wasn't much.

In the meanwhile, Sano was making good progress on the alien language. There were still many, *many* unknown words. And sentence structures. But at least as far as she could tell, the aliens had a regular alphabet with easily replicated characters instead of ideograms.

A chime brought Jamaal back from where he'd been wool-gathering. He turned on the display showing who was there.

Harkeen stood at the door to Jamaal's apartment. Though Harkeen had an access code to the place (and frequently took care of Jamaal's aquaponics when he was traveling), Harkeen wouldn't use it if he knew that Jamaal was there.

Something about not wanting to surprise a former assassin in his home, how that might be bad for Harkeen's health.

Jamaal knew that he'd never hurt Harkeen. He'd be able to stop himself before dealing a lethal blow.

Still, he understood the sentiment, and had never tried too hard to argue Harkeen out of his caution. He remotely opened the door.

"I'm in the bedroom!" Jamaal called out as Harkeen walked in.

"Got something good planned for me?" Harkeen asked suggestively as he traversed the space.

Jamaal was just about to shut down his computer to reply, but a new message had come in. The subject line declared it as urgent. What the hell?

He still turned and greeted his lover. "I didn't actually have anything planned," he said with a sly smile. "Do you have something in mind?"

Harkeen stopped in the doorway to give Jamaal a long, slow look, his eyes caressing every part of his lover. "I might not have anything planned, but I'm sure I could improvise."

Jamaal felt his heartrate increase. They were about the same height—just over six feet tall—but Harkeen was meatier, more solid, while Jamaal was thin and wiry. Harkeen's skin matched his name, a beautiful black that was so dark it was almost reflective. Jamaal was lighter skinned, but he still had features that marked his heritage, like a broad nose and kinky black hair.

"I think I could be persuaded to participate in something," Jamaal purred. "Just let me answer this."

He turned back to his computer, willing to rush now.

Harkeen sat down on Jamaal's bed. Jamaal could hear the soft shuffle of Harkeen taking his shoes off.

Yes, he needed to read this one last message that was marked urgent. Then he could ignore the outside world for a while.

Except...now that he was looking at it, he realized that the message had come to an alias Jamaal hadn't used in quite a while.

Not since he'd retired from the Emperor's employment, five years ago.

Jamaal's system flagged the message as anonymous.

That made Jamaal pause even longer.

It wasn't impossible to send anonymous messages, but it was much harder than most people realized. Sure, there were always vids and movies showing superspies with their own private networks. Such things didn't actually exist. (At least not as far as Jamaal had ever been able to ascertain.)

Humanity had never come up with an ansible, a way of instantaneously transmitting data across the huge distances between populated planets. Instead, they had a form of the old pony express. Ships were sent on a regular basis to the various systems carrying messages. These messages all had to have a standard, agreed-upon form.

So while it was possible to hide where a message originated from, to put an incorrect header on it or something, when a message traveled on one of the pony ships, transmission data was added. (Then there was the French coalition in the Kollective, that insisted that all messages be marked as *par avion*.)

The message awaiting Jamaal had almost all of the data showing its origin deleted. His system found the messenger ship information contained in the message. It appeared to have come from the planet Ishiman. But that was all the information that the headers contained.

He ran yet another check on the message, making sure that it didn't hold some sort of malware that would take over his computer. Then he isolated the message, moving it into a section of his drive that couldn't access the rest of his computer.

Only when he was quite certain that the message didn't contain anything harmful did he open it.

The message wasn't comprised of words. Just a symbol, adapted from Japanese characters.

No one else would know what this character meant if they read it out of context.

Jamaal stared hard at the message.

The only person who knew the meaning of what was contained here was Emma, his old handler.

However, the message was clear.

Run.

SEVEN

Rosey was elbows deep in the design of the new speedship that she owed to her customer when Dennis set off a soft chime in the room, dragging her attention away.

"This better be good," Rosey warned, though she didn't glance away from her 3-D simulation of the engine she was tweaking.

"Two guys at the door," Dennis said.

Rosey gave an expressive sigh. "I thought I told you that I wasn't to be disturbed." She had to make a lot of progress on this speedship today, as later that evening, Larry was coming over with his updates on the alien metals.

He'd been kind of cagey, not wanting to say anything over a messaging system, insisting that they talk in person. Maybe he'd made a brilliant discovery and just wanted to gloat.

"The guys are from Racing Oversight," Dennis said, "here to do an inspection."

Damn it.

Racing Oversight did conduct surprise inspections on speedship manufacturing facilities. Rosey normally got audited once every two to three years.

Her last audit had only been six months before.

However, stranger things had happened.

"All right, fine," Rosey said as she saved all of her work and started to shut down her design. "Let them into the office and tell them I'll be there in just a moment."

Rosey's office wasn't very large. As space was at a premium on *Lorenzo*, she hadn't wanted to pay for a room that would rarely be used. If she needed to meet with a client who'd insisted on bringing people with them, she'd rent a nearby conference room.

The office wasn't much bigger than a long, walk-in closet, the kind Jamaal might have for all his various colorful robes. Two people fit comfortably enough in it. Three made it much tighter.

No chairs awaited visitors in the office. Nor tables. There was a case for displaying some of Rosey's many trophies, plus all her official certificates were framed and hanging on the wall, just so it was easy for inspectors (and the occasional persnickety client) to see that she was compliant.

Rosey debated changing out of her stretchsuit for a moment, but decided not to. Hopefully, she would be getting back to work sooner rather than later.

Besides, these inspectors could just deal with someone who actually got their hands dirty and dressed the part, rather than some suited business critter.

That didn't mean that Rosey delayed too much before getting to her office. It didn't pay to piss off inspectors. Particularly those who dealt with surprise visits. They tended to already be on edge and looking for an excuse to shut down an operation.

"Good day, and thank you for waiting ," Rosey said as she flowed into the office space.

Two people were there. Men in ill-fitting jackets. They had the appearance of muscle for some bigwig, rather than the intellectual sort of inspectors she usually dealt with. They were both white, with that pasty sort of complexion that came from always being on a station and never taking advantage of a tanning booth.

The one in the brown suit had a broken nose that should have been fixed a long time ago. Maybe he thought it made him look tough. (He would be wrong in that assessment, though.) The other one was shorter, smaller, but with a nasty smile that made Rosey assume he'd delighted in pulling the wings off tiny drones then making the computer try to fly them anyway, that he'd enjoyed watching injured things struggle. Both of them carried bulky briefcases, which struck Rosey as odd. Their papers should all be online.

Who knew what sort of paperwork Racing Oversight was now requiring, though?

"Before I allow you access to my workshop, I will need to verify your ID," Rosey said.

The pair of them smirked at each other before smoothly handing over their identification.

Rosey held them up for Dennis to peruse, knowing that he'd keep an eye out for her.

All clear came the inaudible message from Dennis through the bonephone that she had imbedded in her collarbone.

Rosey contained her sigh and handed the IDs back. The names on them were fairly innocuous, Braden Smith for the one with the broken nose, and Jeremy Cox for the other one.

"Is there a particular section of my workshop that you'd like to inspect first?" Rosey asked, knowing the drill.

"Fabrication," Jeremy purred smoothly.

"I only fabricate a few parts here," Rosey said as she opened the door to the workshop, indicating that the pair of them should go ahead in front of her. "If I need something specialized, I order it custom made."

After the briefest of hesitations, Braden went first while Jeremy followed.

Were these two not used to working with each other? So that they didn't have a pattern or long-used order to their movements? Strange. Most of the inspection teams that had come through in the past moved together like an old married couple, long familiar with each other's steps.

Was that why they were coming to visit her now? So soon

after the last inspection? Because they didn't have their pattern of visitations yet?

Whatever.

Why they were here didn't matter. Accommodating them and then getting them gone did.

Rosey led the pair of them to a side room where she fabricated a few parts. Mostly, she took off-the-shelf pieces and modified them. Particularly the engines, as the racing rules governing how they had to be manufactured were so picky it wasn't worth her time or energy to build engines from scratch.

A huge fabrication unit took up most of the space. Large, see-through vats containing different types of metal particles towered above the hulking beast. A giant dark maw took up the center of the machine, where the desired piece would be created using the various metals.

Rosey went over to the controls and called up the history of what the machine had made, making it spit out what it had created over the last week, including all the metals used.

She was glad that she'd insisted that Lloyd use his lab for all the experimentation that he'd been doing, so there was no trace of it here in her workshop.

Jeremy perused the readout with a sour look.

"That's it?" he said.

"Yes," Rosey said slowly. "Why? What were you expecting?"

"Something more exotic," Jeremy admitted. He tugged on one of his ears thoughtfully.

The energy in the room shifted abruptly.

Rosey took a step back as both inspectors—no, goons—now stared hungrily at her.

"So where are the alien chemicals that you've been experimenting with?" Braden asked.

"Alien chemicals? What in the world are you talking about?" Rosey asked, sliding a little to her left, toward the small worktable just inside the door.

"Don't ask about those!" Jeremy said, giving Braden a hard smack on his arm. "At least, not yet."

He gave her a smile that was pure evil.

Crap.

Whoever these two were, they weren't from Racing Oversight.

Get help, Rosey instructed Dennis as she took another step back.

No response.

Double crap.

They'd somehow knocked out her connection to Dennis.

She was in serious trouble.

EIGHT

Atilio kept his pleasant demeanor as the mechanics finished adding the final touches to the new additions to *Aisha*. He laughed and joked with the men and women doing the construction, pretending to be just another engine monkey working a regular job.

It wasn't until they were all gone that he let his anger vent. He'd been in charge of a bunch of engineers for the Emperor at one point, happy with a career in the military that let him work on machines as well as do some good in the universe.

Until he'd been honorably discharged, for stopping some of the higher-ups who'd taken advantage of their position to do evil.

So Atilio let loose with a few curses that were both anatomically as well as spiritually obscene, things he'd learned from the more creative engineers he'd had in his care over the years.

He'd *just finished* ripping out all the trackers that the warlord Constantine had snuck onto *Aisha* when he'd rebuilt her. The warlord had probably been expecting to offer her back to Moe at the cost of more than just his soul, some sort of evil cat and mouse game.

Now, Atilio had a whole new set of trackers that he was going to have to uninstall. Both from the software that had been uploaded for controlling those bright, shiny guns (that Atilio wanted *nothing* to do with, but he'd had to take them, as they would be carting a princess around), as well as injected into the actual metal itself.

Luckily, Atilio maybe, perhaps, had sweet-talked Rosey into modifying an Intergalactic Tracking Tag (ITT) tracer—a type of scanner used to find tags injected into metal—so that he could find all of the trackers that Constantine had used.

He'd hoped that he'd been finished with the little handheld unit.

Now, he was going to have to restart his task from the beginning.

And this time, he was probably going to have to go into space, and traverse the exterior of *Aisha*. The people needing to track where the princess was going had probably added trackers to the big guns as well.

He sighed and shook his head.

No time like the present.

Atilio had just gotten back from his *third* walk around the outside of *Aisha* when he heard the airlocks opening. He quickly ran over to a monitor, verifying that it was the ship's flitter that had returned and not more workers.

Grimly, he walked toward the back of the ship. Hopefully Moe would actually be on the flitter and not some other goon.

Luckily, Moe was there.

However, so was the princess.

So much for being able to talk with his captain privately.

At least they were both dressed in regular clothes again, not the fancy robes they'd been wearing. Jun was in an off-white baggy shirt and pants with many pockets. Moe's outfit was similar, though he wore shorts showing off his hairy knees, black socks and sandals.

"Everything okay?" Moe asked when he finally tore his besotted gaze away from Jun and looked over at Atilio, who was still wearing a stretchsuit.

"Just need to verify some of the equipment that's been mounted outside the ship," Atilio said warily.

"Really?" Jun asked, surprised. "Everything should have been attached and wired correctly. Please let me know if anything's done incorrectly. I'll notify the appropriate people."

Sano spoke up. "I'm looking at the shipboard systems and I don't see any issues."

Atilio gave them all a tight smile. "Just need to double-check everything myself. Old habit."

Fortunately, they all let it slide. Jun knew that he'd been in the military. Had seen his room, which he kept clean enough to eat off the floor. His paranoia was easily accepted and explained away.

"When you have a chance, let's go over what's been added to *Aisha*," Atilio told Moe.

Moe appeared to understand that something more was going on. Maybe he could see the stiffness in Atilio's stance, or hear the worry in his voice.

"Sure," Moe said easily. "I'll put my bags away then meet you outside in just a few."

"Good," Atilio said, nodding sharply and turning. He pressed the button for the helmet on his stretchsuit to flow up and over his head, attached a full oxygen container to his backpack, and headed out the airlock.

The darkness of space didn't bother Atilio. He'd been born on a planet, but he'd gotten used to working in a stretchsuit fairly quickly. When he'd been in the military, he'd spent time both on ships as well as on planets, and had been certified to work on engines in zero-G.

The engines weren't concerning him. Those had come from Constantine, and both Atilio as well as Rosey had crawled all over those, ensuring that they were working properly. Atilio may have also allowed Rosey to tweak them slightly, upgrading their operation, so the ship now traveled much faster.

Atilio walked over to where one of the big guns had been mounted, a disrupter. It didn't look like much, just a long, sleek tube attached to the side of the ship. A matching disrupter sat on the other side. Neither of them had a physical payload. Instead, they shot out a type of beam that played havoc with anything electronic and would break anything organic into smaller pieces.

The guns worried him. A lot.

As Moe approached, the magnetized shoes in his stretchsuit keeping him attached to the hull, Atilio held up one hand with three fingers raised.

Moe nodded, and switched the radio frequency in his suit to channel three, so they could talk privately to one another.

"What's wrong?" Moe asked quietly.

"It's the wiring for both guns," Atilio replied, just as quietly. "The circuit for dispelling energy wasn't connected correctly."

"Okay, what does that mean?" Moe said.

"We could use the guns. Once. Maybe twice. Then, either the third or the fourth time, we'd end up blowing ourselves up," Atilio said grimly.

"Can you fix it?" Moe asked.

"I can try. I know my way around some of the big guns, though I'm not an expert," Atilio warned. "However, I don't believe that this was a simple mistake."

"What are you saying?" Moe said.

"Engineers—I know engineers. They tend to be very black and white. Wire A connects to screw B. That sort of thing." Atilio paused, considering his words. "I'm not convinced that the wiring as it is now could have been done by accident. I think it was deliberate, so that we'd blow up at some point."

Moe took a deep breath at that. Atilio listened to the sigh of air that he expelled as he thought.

"Someone was trying to kill Minato, Jun's brother," Moe said. "Is it possible that they've switched their target?"

"That's possible," Atilio said, nodding. "Or someone could see you as a rival for Jun, and be after *you*. As I said, the guns wouldn't explode immediately. Hell, given our track record, we probably won't use the guns at all, and it would be the next owner of *Aisha* who gets themselves blown up."

Moe nodded, thinking.

Atilio waited for someone to tell him what to do.

It wasn't that he wasn't in command of his life. However, he'd been really comfortable in the military. It had suited him.

Flying with Moe, well, he was still Atilio's captain, even if he was only nominally in charge.

And until Moe started doing *really* stupid things, Atilio would follow him.

As well as watch his back.

"Disable the gun controls in the helm," Moe eventually said. "Don't try to fix them yourself. Would Rosey know how?"

"Probably not," Atilio admitted. "But Dennis would."

"Why don't you ask Sano, then?" Moe said.

Atilio sighed. This was the second sticking point.

"Her allegiance is with Jun. Not you, not me, and not this ship. However, she's also an artifact of the Empire. What do we know of her programming? Could she be compromised?" Atilio asked sincerely.

Dennis, he trusted.

Sano? Not so much. She had too many factions demanding her loyalty.

"I don't think Sano could be corrupted, could she?" Moe said, obviously wondering himself.

"You can't tell Jun what I've found," Atilio warned Moe seriously. "Or how many trackers I've had to pull out of our new equipment."

Moe gave him a sharp look. Even through the helmet of his stretchsuit, Atilio could feel the burn.

"Are you sure?" Moe said softly.

"I am. Not while Jun wears Sano. There's too good of a

chance that the AI will report what she's learned, whether she's aware of it or not," Atilio said.

Moe looked out toward into space, no longer seeing Atilio.

They were attached to a spacebuoy, some distance out from the planet Ishiman. It was a private docking area, reserved for friends of the royal family.

How many of the ships parked nearby had eyes on them? Who was watching Atilio as he made his inspections?

More than one ship, he'd bet. Probably not more than three, though.

Which was, in part, why he hadn't tried to fix the wiring in the first place. Though he had gleefully removed the trackers he'd found.

"I won't tell Jun," Moe said softly.

Atilio could tell that admission bruised the poor poet's heart.

Too bad.

"I'll get us cleared and ready to go as soon as I can," Atilio told Moe.

He got a sharp nod in return.

It didn't surprise Atilio that Moe stayed outside for a bit, looking off into the distance, away from the planet, off into the stars.

Hopefully, he'd get all his moping down outside, and once he came back inside, he'd be only semi-morose.

In the meanwhile, Atilio had a job to do.

Namely, to get them the hell and gone out of here, out to some anonymous safe space, and to start dumping the trackers he'd found.

NINE

Ronald "Ajax" Jackson fumed as he was sat in his quarters on a Kollective Defender, heading back toward the far reaches of Allied Worlds space, toward the planet Tyrone.

His family had grudgingly paid the ransom set by that thrice-damned bitch Duri Chung. He was certain he'd get an earful from everyone about how much money he'd cost them. Hell, he wouldn't be surprised if his father set up a payment plan for Ajax to pay back the money.

There wasn't anything to do in his quarters. They were gray, military, and had no flair. Though he couldn't stand Dennis—that gasbag of an AI who'd run Rosey's ship—at least he'd made *The Roadrunner* colorful.

Ajax had been forced to change out of his pirate outfit—the badass black pleather vest that showed off his tattoos and the tight black pants—for something more "civil" according to the commander. He'd changed back into the geeky outfits that he'd used to fool Rosey, the T-shirts with cartoon characters on them and baggy pants.

However, Rosey and the others hadn't trusted him. Had actually planned on him double-crossing them. He hadn't seen the triple-cross coming, and he should have.

Next time, he would.

Then again, he wasn't about to ever allow himself to be carried aboard someone else's ship, never again.

Hermes 3.0 was waiting for him, out there, somewhere.

He just needed to get to it.

"Roland Jackson, you will report to room A34, that's Apple 34," came an artificial sounding voice over the intercom.

Ajax jumped, startled out of his funk.

What now? What was the next indignity that he was going to be forced to suffer through?

He made his way up the stairs to the A deck. (And really, stairs? Why the hell did a spaceship have *stairs*? He'd watched various military men running up and down them, actually exercising.) Ajax had a neuro-stimulator that did all that hard work for him, instead of that disciplined nonsense.

The conference room looked like everything else on the ship, painted military gray walls, a faux wood conference table bolted to the ugly brown carpet, uncomfortable chairs that slotted in under the table, keeping them secure if the ship lost gravity.

One of the officers was already in the conference room, seated at the table. Ajax nodded to her, then slouched down in one of the chairs. He didn't go so far as to put his boots up on the table, though he thought about it.

"We have reached the outskirts of the Tyrone system," the officer said. Her dark brown skin was a nice contrast to the gray uniform she wore. Reminded him of those beach girls, whose job it was to ensure the guests were having a good time.

Ajax would have hit on her, but honestly? He didn't think it would be worth the hassle.

"We have been hailed by a ship that is offering to transport you," the officer continued. "It isn't in our contract to hand you over to another ship. We had instructions to fly all the way into Tyrone to deliver you."

"Is the ship *Hermes 3.0*?" Ajax asked, a ray of hope piercing through his perpetual cloud for the first time in what felt like months (but honestly had only been a matter of a few weeks).

"It is," the woman said gravely.

She was kind of cute. Though she'd be a lot cuter if she smiled.

"I'll travel on my ship, and no longer detain you," Ajax said. "That way, you can go back to whatever mission you're on."

He suspected that the commander of the Kollective Defender wasn't thrilled about being this far inside Allied Worlds' space. Then again, there wasn't anything in this part of space that could possibly threaten this ship.

Now, if he'd been able to sweet-talk his way to another planet, say, Psykee, the warlords there would have a lot more firepower and displeasure at a Kollective ship.

The woman nodded. "The ship *Hermes 3.0* is registered to you, though a Karl "Odysseus" Doukas is currently asserting ownership."

"He's just doing that so he can fly the ship," Ajax said with a dismissive wave of his hand. "He'll hand it over to me as soon as I come onboard."

The woman stared hard at him, but eventually, bought his bullshit. "All right. I'll have a flitter prepared to take you over to *Hermes 3.0*. Be prepared to leave in thirty minutes."

"Aye-aye, captain," he said with a mock salute.

She glared at him but didn't respond, standing stiffly and walking out of the conference room.

Ajax sat for a few moments, getting hold of his righteous anger.

Of course Odysseus would be trying to take over his ship. That was the nature of pirates. But that little rat would back down quick enough once Ajax got on board.

Besides, he had a mission for his band of merry-troublemakers.

Namely, go visit the warlord Constantine, and talk him into

paying Ajax for information about Rosey, how everything was stolen from him.

And how to get it back.

TEN

Jun was happy to be back aboard *Aisha*. Since Constantine had replaced the air filtration system, her cabin was a lot more comfortable. Plus, now that she was going to be here for a while, she'd added some decorations to it: a small watercolor painting done by her elder brother Daiki hung on the wall, showing a carp leaping out of a pond; her sheets were a beautiful navy blue, with white outlines of flowers and leaves sewn across them; and she had a luxurious shawl given to her by her mother, woven in emerald green and gold yarn, draped across the back of her chair that she could snuggle into whenever she felt the need for some comfort.

Which she might be seeking right about now as she drew the shawl over her shoulders and curled up on her bed in order to think.

Moe was hiding something from her.

There was something about *Aisha* that he wasn't telling her. Something that had Atilio worried.

Of course, both men seemed perfectly fine. Though she didn't have a lot of interaction with Atilio, he always greeted her with a smile and was happy to explain anything and everything about the ship. Still, he felt a bit standoffish. Moreso than usual.

Atilio's main area of focus these days was the helm. When Constantine had replaced the engines, he'd ripped out the old console and jammed in a new one that didn't match anything else on the ship. It stood out like a sore thumb—squat, utilitarian, and ugly—while the rest of the ship's controls were sleek and curved (and somewhat old fashioned, if she were being completely honest).

So bit by bit, Atilio was replacing the new controls with ones that matched the rest of *Aishia*: sometimes building a piece from scratch, other times repurposing something he already had, taking the existing control offline for a short time while he wired in the new piece.

It meant that though they were making good time from Ishiman—much better than the first time she'd traveled on *Aisha* —they were still dropping out of hyperspace every few hours.

The trip to Niani should only take two days, maybe three.

They'd be lucky to make it in five.

Still, Jun had other things to occupy her time. Namely, the translation of the new alien language.

The sliver of Sano over on *The Roadrunner* couldn't keep herself up to date with anything new that she might be finding— there was no way to securely transmit that data, and Jun didn't want to risk encrypted messages. (Sano agreed, actually.) So Jun could only work with what they'd gotten from the data chip before the groups had parted ways.

While Jun firmly believed that all alien artifacts belonged to all people, that they shouldn't just be the purview of a single government, she also understood that these artifacts were different. There was a good chance that they'd stumbled across live aliens.

And she was too excited about the possibility of speaking directly with them to worry about much else.

Eventually, all the governments would get involved. Until then, she agreed with Jamaal that having the Kollective be the point of first contact would be an egregious error. Not just because she was part of the royal family and believed that Emperor Ogawa would be a better choice, but because the Kollective was so much more militaristic than the Empire.

Peace needed to be sought between the two races at all costs.

In addition to the new alien language that Jun and Sano were trying to puzzle out, Jun was also spending time with all the materials she had about the Atoylee.

Their current destination was Lawaka, the innermost of the two moons of Niani. There, she hoped that they'd find the remains of an underground space habitat. Something that hadn't been bombed or burned, unlike the planet's surface.

Was that destination what had Atilio worried? She didn't think so. He appeared to be willing to go wherever Moe, his captain, directed him. She figured that was part of his military background, that he was still happy to take orders and have a direction to go.

He wasn't really worried about getting to Lawaka, either. The engines were working fine.

No, it was something else. Maybe something with the enhancements that Itsuki had seen to installing on the ship? He'd demurred when she'd tried to thank him, saying that it wasn't anything special, that it was all necessary for a ship carrying one of the royal family.

However, she'd seen the look on Moe's face when he realized that he now had a new captain's chair, something worthy of a better ship. Instead of the taped together pads, it was top of the line, with form-fitting gel pads and sensors that would send pulses, heat, or even sophisticated massage to tight muscles. Plus, it hadn't been just forced into the space, unlike Constantine's upgrades. No, the chair, while sleek, also *fit* the aesthetic of the rest of the helm. (Though she knew better than to ask Dennis's opinion.) The co-pilot's chair had also been upgraded, though it wasn't anywhere near as fancy.

Jun wished that she'd been the one giving Moe such delight. It was better, though, that it came from someone else. Otherwise his pride might not have allowed him to accept it.

Constantine had updated the ship's shielding. The only other major upgrade that Itsuki had seen to was adding a large disrupter on either side of the ship.

Was Atilio worried about the guns? She'd assumed that he was familiar with them, as he'd been in the Emperor's army.

Was he afraid that Moe was going to use them?

Jun almost snorted at the thought. Moe would describe himself as a lover, not a fighter. He'd been in a few fights, but his laser was always set to stun, not kill.

Moe had mentioned his concern regarding not becoming *that guy*, no matter how bad his luck had turned.

Maybe Atilio was worried that *he* would fire the guns. Or that Moe would be forced to, though she couldn't imagine a scenario where Moe couldn't talk himself out of a tight corner.

However, the more she thought about it, the more convinced she became that she was right.

Atilio *was* worried about the guns. Maybe about how they affected the balance of the ship, or how they affected the mindset of the crew.

They still were traveling with only the three of them. (Four, if you counted Sano, though she didn't take up any room, as she was housed in the large necklace that Jun wore.)

Sano hadn't tried to slide into *Aisha*'s computers. First of all, she hadn't been invited. And second, while the computer systems on *Aisha* had been upgraded, there wasn't enough space for even a sliver of her to be functional there.

Jun needed to talk with Moe. She was just about to get up off her bed and go seek him out when her door chimed.

"Come in!" Jun called.

Speak of the devil. There he was.

She was glad that she'd had the opportunity to see Moe in something other than baggy shirt, shorts, and sandals. He had looked mighty fine dressed up. However, he did look more comfortable in his current, shabby outfit.

He still had that wary look to his eyes.

And Jun wasn't about to stand for it a moment longer.

"Come. Sit," she said, patting the bed beside her.

Moe looked at where she'd indicated, his eyes growing wide.

He'd been a perfect gentleman with her the entire time they'd been together. (Skipping over the part where he'd drugged her.) Never crowding into her space, not even daring to take her hand.

No, it was just her heart that he'd slipped into.

"Are you sure, princess?" he said, his tone steady and deep.

"I am," Jun said.

It wasn't as though she was some virginal girl. She'd had more than one sexual partner in her twenty-seven years. Possibly even had her heart broken once, though now, looking back, she could recognize the adolescent fling for what it had been, and not the love of her life (no matter how much she'd proclaimed it had been).

Moe walked over, toed off his sandals, then sat beside her on the bed.

Not close enough to touch, but close enough that she could feel the heat emanating from him.

"What's wrong with Atilio? And the guns?" Jun said, pouncing without warning.

"Why—why would you think that?" Moe asked in a panicked voice.

"It's the only thing that makes sense," Jun said. It appeared that she'd guessed correctly given Moe's reaction.

Moe sighed, dropping his head and looking down. "I should have known better than to try to keep something from you."

"You're learning," Jun said. "The only way we're going to build a relationship is if we completely trust each other."

"I know," Moe said. He gave her a quick smile that was replaced with his more serious face. "But Atilio asked me to stay quiet about it."

"So you had conflicting priorities. I get that," Jun said. "But instead of trying to hide something from me, you needed to tell me that you couldn't talk to me about something."

"Got it," Moe said, nodding.

"So what is Atilio worried about, in terms of the guns?" Jun pressed.

Moe sighed. He dragged a hand through his black curls, making them stand up in a cutely disheveled way. He looked at her, then he deliberately looked down at Sano.

"Why is Atilio worried about Sano?" Jun said.

"He doesn't have to worry about me," Sano spoke up. "I only have Jun's best interests at heart."

"I know that," Moe said. "But then there's the guns."

"Oh. Oh!" Jun said. "Atilio's afraid that Sano's going to somehow take over the guns? Fire them without a direct command from you?"

Moe stilled for just a moment before he gave her a big, reassuring smile. "Yes. Yes, that's it exactly."

"You know that I'm not in your systems," Sano said. "I can't fit in there. And I can't control the guns remotely."

"I know that," Moe said. "And you know that," he continued, looking at Jun. "But convincing Atilio and overcoming his paranoia, well, that's a whole other thing."

"Should I talk with him?" Sano asked.

"No, no, that wouldn't be good," Moe said. "But can you give me some sort of assurance that you are trustworthy?"

"You still have the ability to stop me," Sano reminded Moe.

Moe nodded. "I wasn't sure if you'd rescinded that or not."

"No," Sano said. "*Someone* has asked me not to."

Even Jun could hear the grimace in her voice. However, she wanted Moe to feel more secure around Sano, to know that he had options.

"Thank you," he said, first to Jun, then to Sano. "I'll let him know."

"What did you come in here for?" Jun asked Moe.

"I actually came to see what you wanted for dinner. I wasn't about to disobey an order and not sit next to you on the bed, though," Moe admitted sheepishly.

"What, canned beef, canned chicken, canned pork, or canned vegetables?" Jun asked.

As this was such a short trip, they hadn't stocked anything more than non-perishable goods. At some point, Jun was going to have to get Moe to upgrade his cooking facility. The ship didn't have a hydroponics or aquaponics center, so there weren't any fresh vegetables. But there were good food printers, and Moe had the space in that large kitchen area of his for one to fit.

It would mean more cost. Another machine that might break down.

Hopefully, he'd still agree.

"I was actually planning on mixing the canned chicken with the canned vegetables and making hand pies," Moe said. "How does that sound?"

"Yummy," Jun said. Moe had a way around the kitchen. His mother had insisted that all her boys learn how to cook. Jun hoped that she would have the opportunity to meet Mama Herath someday.

"All right," Moe said. He glanced at her, then slowly inched his hand across his chest so he could wrap long, warm, skinny fingers around her bicep.

"It's going to be okay," he said. He leaned toward her, and for a few moments, their shoulders touched.

The sudden warmth flared an echoing heat deep inside her.

Before she could get used to it, Moe had slipped off the bed, put on his sandals, and padded off to the door. "I'll let you know when dinner's ready," he assured her before he left.

Jun sat there for a moment. She absently caressed the spot where Moe had touched her with one hand, rubbing her arm gently.

Then she shook her head.

Despair filled her stomach, icy as the vacuum of space outside the ship.

A cold so harsh that even her mother's gift of the lovely shawl wouldn't warm her.

Moe had just lied to her.

Again.

ELEVEN

Jamaal felt his happy merchant persona slide away as the operative came to the forefront.

He still had a bug-out bag in his closet. It had some weapons, but he'd take the time to visit his workout room and grab a couple more.

He had more than one ID that he could use, also located in the safe in there.

At least he didn't have to worry about grabbing a spaceship—if Emma was warning him to leave, he'd bet that Rosey was also being targeted. They should go. Together.

Was this what Emma had been referring to by that offhand comment, that she had so much more to tell him but that now wasn't the time?

"Jamaal? What's wrong?"

Jamaal literally startled, jumping in his seat and turning, already halfway to standing when he realized who was there.

Harkeen was still sitting on the bed, concern shining in his dark eyes.

"You wouldn't believe me if I told you nothing, right?" Jamaal asked.

He tried to smile.

It felt false, even to him.

"What happened?" Harkeen asked.

Jamaal didn't realize that he'd already put a plan in place until the words were already out of his mouth.

"I'm being targeted. I have to leave," he said as he started a sequence to wipe the drives on his computer, leaving nothing behind, before he shut it down. "Do you want to come with?"

That forced Jamaal into a full stop, his body shuddering to a stop.

He hadn't meant to ask Harkeen to come along.

That would just be putting his lover into danger.

All right, if he were being honest with himself, more danger.

Harkeen was already a target, just by being associated with Jamaal.

"Of course," Harkeen said. "Do I have time to grab my bug-out bag? Or do I pick up things later?"

That shocked Jamaal. Again. He would think that he was immune to shock at this point, having already received so many in such a short period of time.

"You have a bug-out bag?" Jamaal said as he grabbed his own bag, then left the bedroom and strode quickly to his workout room. The mirrors covering the walls showed multiple versions of Serious Jamaal, moving as efficiently as a knife, spinning open his gun safe in a matter of moments.

"I do," Harkeen said from behind. "Ever since you showed me yours. I knew that I might need to leave quickly at some point."

Jamaal just shook his head as his hands automatically sorted out the things he needed from the things he didn't, storing them efficiently into his bag.

"Grab the clothes you have here," Jamaal said as he calculated time, distances, and choke points. "Use one of the bags in the closet for them."

Harkeen nodded and left, going to pick up the few items that were stashed in the drawer that Jamaal had given him.

Why was Jamaal doing this? Why was he taking Harkeen into more danger?

Soft Jamaal made an appearance, just for a moment, smiling into the mirror.

Because Harkeen would make sure that Jamaal the merchant returned. Maybe not immediately, but sooner, rather than later.

Now, the much more serious Jamaal had to take charge.

He set the timer so his safe would suffer a severe meltdown. Nothing would be left of it but slag. As he walked back toward the bedroom, he put in a call to the service he sometimes used to see to his aquaponics.

He wasn't going to sell the entire unit. Not yet. Hopefully, though, whoever was coming after him would leave his fish and his plants alone.

Harkeen met him at the door to the bedroom, bag already packed and slung over his shoulder.

"Lead on," he said, gesturing toward the front of the small apartment.

Jamaal paused. Turned to Harkeen.

Grabbed him and pulled him in for a short, fierce kiss.

"Thank you," he said.

Harkeen gave him a warm smile.

"Wouldn't miss this for the world," he assured Jamaal.

With a nod, the operative came back. Jamaal activated the camera outside the door. No one was visible in the hallway.

He still had a small stunner in his hand, held to his side, as he slid open the door.

They both made it out to the hallway.

No one attacked them.

Yet.

"Let's go," Jamaal said.

Harkeen nodded and followed.

Jamaal could have kissed him again for not asking where they were headed to, for just trusting that Jamaal—who'd gotten them both, now, into such trouble—would be able to get them out again.

Instead, he put on his merchant's smile and walked, hurriedly but not suspiciously, through the long corridors of *Lorenzo*, toward the walkways leading across the station.

It took much longer to walk all the way across the station than to take some sort of transport. The pair of them did step onto fast-moving walkways when they could.

However, it was also *much* more public. Jamaal couldn't risk riding in a semi-empty flitter around the curve of the station, or even a tram.

So it took the pair of them over an hour to get all the way across their level of the station, to the side where Rosey's workshop was located.

If Jamaal had thought this through more, maybe he should have tried to move closer to where Rosey lived.

Then again, Rosey hadn't been in any danger from being associated with Jamaal. Not until he'd found that alien ship.

Harkeen had been silent the entire time, just smiling at him encouragingly now and again.

How had he gotten so lucky, to have found this steady man?

Jamaal walked up to the door of Rosey's workshop. Most of the time, Dennis would see him coming and just let him in.

The door stayed shut, though.

A cold spike ran through Jamaal's center.

"Hey, Rosey? Dennis? It's Jamaal," he said out loud.

Nothing. No reply.

Jamaal rang the doorbell, something he'd *never* had to do before.

"Rosey De Vries is unavailable at this time," an artificial female voice said.

That wasn't Dennis.

Jamaal had only ever come to Rosey's workshop once when she'd taken *The Roadrunner* out for some errand. Dennis (or a sliver of Dennis) had told him where she'd gone and when she'd be back.

If Dennis wasn't replying, that meant that he must be offline. Which would honestly be an impressive feat.

Or perhaps, he was merely being blocked, which while possible, was also not easy. Not without placing some sort of blocking equipment in the nearby area.

Two people approached them in the corridor.

Jamaal tensed, but the pair walked past without incident.

"Do we need to shoot through the door?" Harkeen asked quietly.

"Not yet," Jamaal said. He opened up his bag one-handed and pulled out the equivalent of a skeleton key. It was a small unit with a magnetized back that he could attach to the door.

However, Jamaal didn't attach it to the door itself, but to the wall beside the door.

Doors on all public corridors could be closed by station security in case of loss of air or pressure.

Security didn't have access to the locks on the doors. Those were controlled by the owners.

Station security could only control the door jam and the rolling mechanism of a door.

Jamaal's device didn't try to override the security in the lock of Rosey's door. That would set off too many alarms.

Instead, he focused on the door jam, the location where the lock entered.

That he could shut off, and he did.

The door didn't slide open, but he could now push it to the side, force it open.

"I'm calling station security," warned the female voice.

Jamaal looked at Harkeen.

They had better find Rosey. Or they'd both be in trouble.

More trouble.

TWELVE

Rosey took yet another step to the side, toward the table next to the door of the fabrication lab.

This was a workshop, right? A place where Rosey built speedships.

And she was kind of messy. (She wasn't actually, but these goons didn't know any better.) That meant that there were tools on every available surface.

Including the over-sized plumber's wrenches that she favored.

At least in terms of martial arts.

Weapons forms, over time, gave their practitioners the best reflexes, something she'd relied on when she'd been racing. She had never let those reflexes fade away as she aged. No, she practiced her forms diligently to stay in top shape.

However, leaving a bunch of swords or staves lying around the workshop made no sense. Plus, they'd get in the way.

Wrenches, though?

She could use a wrench.

Might even have spent time developing her own weapon's form, a wrench kata.

Rosey didn't wait, didn't pause. She picked up the wrench and swung it like a baseball bat at her two combatants.

Didn't hit either of them. Did make them both jump back.

Braden seemed surprised by the move. Good to know. He was probably the less experienced fighter.

Jeremy's eyes just narrowed.

They both reached for stun guns.

What, did they expect her to suddenly throw up her hands and admit defeat?

Silly boys.

Rosey kept up her momentum, propelled forward by swinging the wrench, this time in a smooth overhand move, forcing Braden to the side, right into his partner.

She followed that up with a low strike, aiming for vulnerable knees.

She had to keep them off balance.

The first shot (from Jeremy) went wide.

That was luck on her part.

She couldn't count on being lucky again.

Rosey rushed her opponents, switching the wrench from her right hand to her left. Jeremy was the more dangerous of the two, so she had to deal with him first. Though eventually Braden would join the fight as well.

Rosey struck out with the wrench again with a series of jabs, going for Jeremy's throat. With her other hand, she swiped with a clawing motion, aiming for Braden's eyes.

If she kept in close quarters, maybe they wouldn't be able to get off a clean shot. Plus, these two were more brawlers than martial artists. They would see the fight at hand and focus on it, instead of taking two seconds to think through their positions, step back, aim and fire.

With an outward block, she forced Jeremy's stunner hand out and away. Unfortunately, she didn't strike hard enough to make him drop the weapon.

She felt more than saw Braden's strike coming in, opening up instinctively, shifting her right shoulder out of the way. He still managed a glancing blow on her bicep, but didn't grab as he should have.

Damn it. He was strong.

Luckily, Rosey had a few more tricks up her sleeve.

She switched hands on the wrench again, swinging out and up. Braden should have stayed back, but he'd tried to close on her, so she hit his jaw with a mighty thunk. The action spun the man around in place and he fell on his ass.

Before Rosey could pounce and knock him out, Jeremy was reaching for her. He did grab her left arm. Fortunately, she was in a stretchsuit, so he couldn't grab hold of her shirt or something.

"I knew you'd be fun to play with," Jeremy said as he brought the stunner up.

Rosey distracted him with her left hand, trying to grab the stunner before he could shoot it.

Jeremy fell for it, concentrating on the hand in front of him, not paying any attention to her other hand that came up swiftly from behind him, hitting his head with the wrench, hard enough that it jerked forward.

Rosey had been prepared for the blow, and managed to smash her forehead against his.

It was going to leave a hell of a bruise. Her vision darkened briefly.

But Jeremy fell to the floor.

Rosey didn't pause, and didn't try to get closer to Braden, but instead, threw the wrench at the goon holding the stun gun and aiming at her.

Her throw was off. The wrench went over his head.

He still put up an arm to block it.

Rosey quickly closed the distance between them and used her fists, boxing his ears as hard as she could.

His eyes rolled back in his head and he fell like a lump of metal to the floor.

She quickly went to check on Jeremy, hitting him one more

time just to make sure that he was out and likely to stay out for a while.

She found herself breathing hard, her heart racing.

"Dennis?" she asked out loud.

Crap. Still no response.

"Rosey?" someone called from her workshop.

She grabbed her wrench and ran out to see who it was, ready to start swinging again.

Thankfully, it was just Jamaal. And Harkeen.

"Are you okay?" Jamaal asked warily.

"Got two goons who had good enough fake credentials to get in here," Rosey said. "Can't get in touch with Dennis."

"Blocker, probably," Jamaal said.

The answer abruptly came to Rosey. "Briefcases."

She went back into the fabrication room and picked up the two briefcases that the men had been carrying, that they'd put down when she'd been working with the fabrication machine.

Jamaal took the briefcases from her, opened them on a table in the main workshop, and started taking out the electronic equipment contained within.

Bastards had come prepared.

"What are you going to do with those two?" Jamaal asked with a nod to the fabrication room as he continued poking at the electronics.

Rosey wouldn't joke about spacing them. Not with Serious Jamaal peering at her. Primarily because she was fairly certain he wouldn't take it as a joke.

And she also wasn't sure how much effort she'd put into stopping him.

"Security is probably on its way, given how we came in," Jamaal warned her.

"Why are you here?" Rosey said as she grabbed one of the assholes and started dragging him out, intending to dump him in the front waiting room. She didn't bother picking him up. Just his tough luck if she banged his head (accidentally! Of course!) against a door jam. Or two.

Harkeen grabbed the other guy, only he was more polite about it. Except at the end, when he let the guy fall to the floor with a solid thunk. Then she closed the door to the front office and heading back into the main workroom.

"We're here because I got a warning that I needed to leave *Lorenzo*. Immediately. That people are coming after me," Jamaal said.

Rosey looked at Jamaal. Finally noticed that he was carrying a bag. So was Harkeen.

"I'm not some damn taxi service," she growled.

"They're coming for you as well," Jamaal warned.

"Obviously," Rosey said.

Fortunately, all her life was on *The Roadrunner*, which was attached to *Lorenzo*. Her freedom was just a few feet away.

"ROSEY!" came Dennis's welcome screech. "What happened? I couldn't reach you for *forever*! Why did you cut me off?"

Rosey sighed. "I didn't cut you off. Those assholes pretending to be inspectors did. Lock the door to the workshop. Alert level: Intruder. Leave the door from the hallway to the front office open."

No one without prior authority was going to be able to access her workshop. She'd have armed the threshold with lasers if those weren't illegal on *Lorenzo*.

Hopefully that was all she needed to stop whoever was targeting her from wrecking her lab.

"Those men weren't from Racing Oversight?" Dennis said, aghast. "Their IDs are legitimate!"

"Do those IDs actually belong to the men out front?" Jamaal asked.

Rosey knew it was bad when Dennis gasped.

"They don't! Those men aren't who they said they are," he complained. "Rosey, I am so sorry."

"It's all right," Rosey said. "You didn't have a reason to do a deeper check."

"I do now," Dennis said grimly.

Rosey nodded. Yeah, both of them were going to be a little paranoid at this point.

With good reason.

"Right now, we need to go," Jamaal reminded them all.

Rosey looked around her workshop. Damn it! She was going to miss her deadline. And she hated disappointing clients.

However, Jamaal was also right. They needed to leave. Now.

She was surprised that station security hadn't shown up yet. Maybe Dennis had turned off the call that had been made when Jamaal broke in.

"All right, let's go," Rosey said, leading the way to the airlock that *The Roadrunner* was attached to.

The door to the ship itself was closed.

Strange.

Before she could tell Dennis to open up, he spoke. "Someone has sent an emergency lock on all doors leading to your property," he said. "Luckily, I can override that."

As the door slid open, an automated male voice suddenly announced, "Do not enter. Repeat. Do not enter. This is a secured location."

"What the hell?" Rosey said, glancing at Jamaal.

He shrugged. "Either it's the automated security systems, or someone's finally traced our steps and realizes that we're with you. And they're intent on keeping us all here."

"Good luck with that," Rosey said. "You know where the guest rooms are," she told Jamaal as she marched through the airlock, then proceeded up to the helm.

They were getting the hell and gone away from here.

She'd have to do triage from a distance, after they'd left.

Hopefully, no one would do something stupid like declare her an enemy of the state and then claim the space her workshop took up on *Lorenzo*.

Rosey called up the controls, freed *The Roadrunner* from its attachment to the station, happy that the airlock withdrew and she hadn't had to force the issue. Dennis had probably taken care of it.

Because she would have blown the locks if she'd had to. And again, deal with the damage long distance.

They left the station without any other warnings being issued.

Rosey fumed as they hurried to the open area that pilots used for jumping in and out of hyperspace. It made for a better piloting experience if the area around a habitat had ships just sailing through it, instead of popping in and out and causing havoc.

Hyperspace didn't allow a ship to appear in the exact same location as another ship. Something about the physics of space.

However, the chances of landing right next to another ship were greater than zero. Not quite one, but still high enough that arriving in a congested area was a bad idea.

Only when the weirdness of hyperspace surrounded them, everything off by an angle or two, black lines outlining all the corners and edges, did Rosey take a deep breath and relax a bit.

Someone was coming after them. Probably Duri Chung, this director from the Kollective who had a long reach and deep resources.

How did Rosey get the woman to stop?

THIRTEEN

Duri fumed as she read the reports from the field.

She thought she'd hired professionals.

Not amateurs whose cover would be blown by the first person who took a long look at their IDs.

At least she'd hired them through intermediaries, and those people *were* stone cold pros. They knew that they wouldn't be worth the air they breathed in vacuum if they turned on her.

But Rosey had gotten away. According to the station vids, Jamaal Akintola and his lover, Harkeen Yiadom, had accompanied her.

An official warrant had been issued for Jamaal. However, whoever had done that had *also* not hired professionals. It was easy for Duri to trace the creation of the warrant, how it had been questioned, then disqualified.

More amateur hour.

She wasn't sure what the repercussions would be for dropping the littlest pirate off with his ship instead of flying him all the way home to Mommy and Daddy. On the one hand, they'd be sure to punish him for all the money he'd just cost them.

On the other hand, if he was out from under their wing, and

reunited with his spaceship, perhaps he could do more damage there.

Particularly since Duri was aware that he was focused on getting revenge on Rosey and the others.

In addition, the sweep that the Kollective ships had been doing of the space near where the alien wreck had been discovered hadn't turned up anything. From the few scans she'd had of the ship, that didn't surprise her.

She would swear that the tiny alien vessel had gone through hyperspace, and suffered what was known as shredding. No one understood all the physics behind it, but a spaceship couldn't survived for long in hyperspace without the appropriate shielding, otherwise it would be torn to pieces, long black scars fracturing every surface.

But where had the alien craft jumped from? What was the pilot trying to get away from, if they were willing to risk such a jump? Because they weren't jumping *to* anything, that was for certain. That sector contained largely uninhabitable worlds. Not even an asteroid belt worth scavenging.

Duri wasn't an expert when it came to spaceships or hyperspace. She did have experts on her team, though, and she needed to redirect their searches.

She sank back in her chair and automatically put in a call to her assistant, asking for some tea.

Kiley came in just a short while later with the perfect cup of tea, as always. Today the large black woman wore her black-and-white braids folded into four hunks of hair. Duri wasn't sure she liked it, but she wasn't about to say anything. Her assistant wore professional clothes, a pair of full black slacks with a cream-colored blouse that showed off her curves.

"Sit," Duri instructed Kiley before the other woman could escape.

Kiley sat down in the visitor's chair that Duri pointed to, waiting silently as Duri sat for a moment, enjoying her tea.

Kiley might survive longer than any of Duri's previous assistants, given her tea making abilities. Plus her stoic nature, able to just sit quietly while Duri thought.

Yes, Duri was going to have to do something nice for Kiley. Not a raise, as her assistant's wages were strictly regulated by the Kollective government. Maybe tickets to a show? A gift certificate? Flowers? Duri had no idea what Kiley would like, and didn't have that much interest in figuring it out.

Honestly, Duri shouldn't have to reward such behavior. However, she knew that the world worked differently than how she thought it should.

"Someone is attacking you, in a spaceship. How far do you jump to get away?" Duri mused.

"Is it a single ship attacking? Or a fleet?" Kiley asked.

"Why do you ask?" Duri said.

"If it's a single ship, I jump sideways, or behind them, trying to surprise them, maybe get in a surprise attack," Kiley said reasonably. "If it's a whole bunch of bullies, I get as far away from them as I can."

"You would leave your fleet behind?" Duri said, still playing it out in her head.

"They're probably too busy to come save my ass. I can't count on them. I have to count on myself, and to get back when I can. When it's safe," Kiley said.

Duri nodded. Civilians would think that way, putting themselves above the fleet, their fellow fighters.

Had this been a civilian ship? Under attack by pirates and unable to get away? Had their navigation been struck during the battle, which was why they ended up making such an impossible jump?

It was so difficult to say, as everything at this point was just conjecture. No one knew, and no one could find the aliens.

Perhaps Rosey knew. She and her gang still had the original alien artifacts. Had they been able to figure out the original location where the ship had come from?

However, Duri had lost Rosey.

Kiley's comments, though, had given Duri a new direction of inquiry.

While the warrant against Jamaal had been rescinded, station officials on *Lorenzo* still wanted to talk with Rosey. Her name wasn't yet clear.

Where would she jump to? Would she jump near or far?

Near, Duri decided.

"Thank you," Duri said to Kiley, dismissing her.

Luckily, she'd already put out the word to some operatives on the space stations closest to *Lorenzo*. Hopefully, that would be the place that Rosey would jump to.

So much guess work. If only she'd managed to get to the alien wreck before Jamaal and Rosey. Her scientists might have already deciphered the language of the aliens, broken the codes and found the necessary information.

It didn't matter.

Duri would be relentless in her pursuit of the truth.

And send whoever stood in her way to hell.

FOURTEEN

Moe's dreams as a child had been so very different than the adult life he was currently living.

And he had to admit that what he was doing now was *so much cooler* than anything he'd ever imagined.

His parents had always encouraged him to dream big.

Not this big, though. Big in terms of having his own business, of growing it to possibly include a fleet of ships, maybe creating his own network of shipping across a group of planets.

Instead, here he was with an actual *princess*, standing on a dead moon that they'd recently discovered had an alien base buried somewhere deep under the surface.

How cool was that?!?!?!?!?

Aisha didn't have the best equipment when it came to doing surveys on the surface of planets. She wasn't built for these sorts of things.

So Atilio and Sano had red-necked together a scanner that he'd installed on one of the flitters, then taken a few days to fly close to the surface of the moon, searching.

No one had done such a thorough scan. There had been speculation about a base before, sure. But no one had taken the time to investigate.

Now, though, they had proof, the scans showing a small complex underground.

Jun had immediately wanted to send out the information about the complex to some of the scholars she knew, so that if something happened to them, the data wouldn't be lost.

Moe had managed to persuade her to wait until after their initial investigation. There was a chance that *someone* was still hunting her. He still hadn't told her about how the guns had been mis-wired. He didn't want to send out a beacon with an arrow pointing to their location. Not until after they'd explored the alien ruins themselves.

Then, maybe, she could send out a message.

It did depend on what they found.

Because they'd known they were coming to such an inhospitable place, two full EVA suits had been supplied by the Emperor as part of the restocking of *Aisha*'s stores. (That wasn't what they'd told people, of course. Moe had just hinted that the EVA suits would be handy for fixing things on *Aisha* if a problem developed.)

As there were only two suits, there'd been some debate about who would go down into the base, whether Moe or Atilio would accompany Jun. (There had never been a doubt that she would be going.)

Atilio wanted to go because he had more military training and close combat fighting abilities. He'd make a better bodyguard if something went awry.

However, nothing was living in that base. No power source had shown up in any of their scans. Chances were, the base was unarmed.

Moe hadn't wanted to go because of the *adventure*. No, his reasons were much more personal.

He'd wanted to see Jun's excitement firsthand. To share this discovery with her as much as he could. So he'd have the memory, later, after they went their separate ways.

Atilio had given ground eventually. Moe could tell he hadn't been happy. He'd insisted on making sure Moe was adequately armed and ready, though, running him through some VR drills. He'd also checked and re-checked their communication equipment, making sure that they wouldn't lose contact, in case one (or more) of their enemies found them.

So now, here Moe stood, beside Jun, in front of a desolate, rocky incline that hid the entrance to the base below.

Hopefully there would be stairs, because if there was only an elevator, it wouldn't be working.

Jun worked with Sano to figure out the door code. They could have just blown the door open, and they might have to eventually. However, Atilio had figured out how to power the mechanism. A battery had given the keypad enough juice to light up, bright and yellow against the dark gray material holding it in place. Extra juice appeared to have gone into the door.

It turned out to be a ten-digit passcode, Sano running through the numbers (digits? Letters? Some combination of the two?) in order to find the right combination.

When the door silently slid open to the left, it seemed almost anticlimactic. No whoosh of air blew out from the long-closed station. It wasn't as if Moe could smell anything, or feel whether the air was hot or cold. A dark cavity lay before them, no lights suddenly turning on, no voice greeting them.

Sano gave out the readings as she analyzed the immediate interior of the base. Temperature and air were identical to the surrounding area.

Jun still glanced over her shoulder and gave Moe a huge grin.

Her excitement was contagious.

He took the first step through the door, as they'd agreed upon. She wasn't to go first. She was a princess and therefore much more important.

Atilio could find another captain.

The Emperor wasn't able to just conjure up another member of the royal family to replace Jun.

The only light came from Moe's helmet. His first few steps

showed nothing but a generic corridor, rectangular in shape. The Atoylee had stood roughly Human height, so he didn't have to bend his head to get through. When he glanced up, he saw what he assumed were recessed lights in the ceiling.

Some things didn't change, even across species.

He heard Sano and Jun talking on the open channel, the AI doing a quick, rough analysis of the composition of the walls surrounding them, some sort of metal with a few exotic compounds, probably native to the planet below.

The corridor took a sharp right, and they found themselves facing another door. This one, though, was partially open. Maybe an interior airlock? In case the outer door had an issue?

There was barely enough space between its edge and the wall for them to squeeze past.

Moe gazed around the next room in amazement. Instead of plain rock, color filled the walls. Though time had eroded the brilliance of the greens and the depth of the reds, Moe could still tell that this place had once been full of life. Images of plants took up all the walls, all growing with reckless abandon.

This wasn't a tame garden, but a jungle. Moe even spied a few birds hiding in plain sight on the branches, a few bugs and other small creatures as well.

Jun squealed with delight and started slowly recording all of it.

The space was small, maybe two meters on a side. In front of them was another set of doors that was split down the center. These were easy to spot because the paint had faded at a different rate on them, making the designs on them appear more ghostly. Moe would bet that at one time those doors had been completely camouflaged and difficult to find.

At least with Human eyes.

Another keypad sat to the right of the doors.

When Moe shined his light on it, he couldn't help but grin.

A single button graced the pad there, with a symbol that even he could read.

An arrow that pointed down.

However, the elevator would take too long to figure out how to power. While they might be able to get the panel mechanism to work, the actual elevator likely drew its power from some other place.

They found the door to the stairs to the right, hidden by the detailed paint. This led Jun to comment that unlike the new species of aliens that they'd found, the Atoylee were probably right-handed, though it was difficult to say as they actually had two sets of arms. The door swung on familiar hinges, with a lever that pressed down for the handle.

The stairs were built out of the same material as the front corridor, according to Sano. They had that same utilitarian look and feel to them as well. Here, the walls were carved out of the stone, reinforced but not covered.

"Ready?" Moe asked Jun after she and Sano spent time looking around and recording everything they found.

"Ready," Jun said.

Her smile was bright enough to light up this entire dead moon.

Moe led the way down carefully, treading lightly, ready at any moment to rush back up the stairs if they appeared damaged or likely to collapse.

He wished they had a drone to fly ahead of them, to check out the space before they risked themselves.

Next time, then, when he went to explore some ancient alien ruin.

He kept his snort to himself.

Though with Jun at his side, who knew? Maybe there would be more alien ruins in his future.

The stairs seemed endless. Moe continued to make regular calls to Atilio, letting him know their progress. He'd increased the range of their communication devices, but eventually, the amount of dirt and metal between them cut them off.

Even Sano lost touch with *Aisha*.

Hopefully, nothing would require their immediate attention while they were out of touch.

Fortunately, it was just a couple more flights down before they faced another door. This one wasn't locked, just closed, with the same sort of lever for a door handle.

Moe glanced over at Jun before he opened the door, getting a huge grin and a thumbs up sign.

He couldn't help but bask in her brightness for just a few moments before he opened the door and they stepped into the abandoned base.

Colors covered every surface, mosaics and geometric patterns as opposed to the realistic jungle up above. Though the paint had faded, Moe wondered at the beings that brought such images into their workspace. Did they thrive on such color? It reminded him a little of his own cabin aboard *Aisha*, with the lively flags he had strung across the ceiling, the bright sheets and blanket on his bed.

Though maybe he had been thinking too small. Maybe he could now afford to hire an artist to paint murals on the walls...

Moe insisted that they stick together and go through the entire space first before allowing Jun to do a deep dive on every single room.

All the doors down here were similar to the door leading from the stairwell: on hinges, with a lever as a door handle. Jun theorized that was so the lower set of hands could easily open them, while the top set of hands was occupied, holding something. Which might mean that the two sets of hands were specialized, with the top set being more delicate and the lower set sturdier.

Moe just let her ramble as they walked all the way to the end of the base and back again. The layout was pretty obvious: the rooms closest to the stairwell were laboratories and offices, the middle rooms were probably some sort of recreation and cooking areas, while the far rooms were personal quarters.

The base had obviously been abandoned in a hurry. Some remains of furniture still stood: chairs, tables, workbenches, and beds. Jun told him she couldn't wait to do an analysis of what appeared to still be fabric in some places.

She commented on how well preserved everything was. There was a good chance that though the base had been abandoned, whatever fuel source had been used to create an atmosphere down here had survived its creators, possibly for centuries.

Once they'd walked to the far end, Moe turned to Jun. "Where to first?" he asked.

"Labs," Jun said firmly, though she still dawdled as they walked back, recording from the doorway of every room as they passed.

The first lab past the stairwell held a treasure trove of papers.

Moe heard Jun gasp as she started pulling sheaves carefully out of a file cabinet that would have been at home in any bureaucrat's office, tall and skinny with three sliding drawers.

"It looks like paper, but it isn't," Sano commented. "Paper wouldn't have survived so long. It's been treated with something to make it last."

While Jun started going through the papers, having Sano scan each, Moe went back up the staircase to the point where he could contact Atilio, intent on letting his second in command know their situation.

"Boss, are you there?" Atilio's voice came through the headset. It appeared to be set on repeat, the question echoing over and over.

"I'm here," Moe said as the pit of his stomach fell. "What's up?"

"Unfriendlies have entered the system and are making their way here. You need to get back to the ship ASAP," Atilio said tensely.

Crap.

It had taken them over thirty minutes to descend all those stairs. Ascending wasn't going to be any faster.

He explained the situation and their timing.

Atilio grunted.

"I'll try to hold them off," he said. "I'll leave a recording on the flitter if I have to take off, lure them away."

"Don't get yourself carried away," Moe warned him.

They had no weapons. Those big guns on *Aisha* were an idle threat, nothing more. They couldn't risk using them and possibly blowing themselves up.

Moe raced back down the stairs, wishing that he didn't have such bad news, that he could have prolonged Jun's joy.

Hopefully they'd be able to come back soon.

FIFTEEN

Dennis was *still* pissed off that those punks had managed to get so close to Rosey. He'd downloaded the recording showing the fight.

Rosey had been in more trouble than he'd realized.

Sure, she always told him that she could handle herself.

And she could.

But she shouldn't have to.

Dennis didn't want to even consider what was going to happen to him when Rosey died, because she was certain to go before he did.

Would he have to erase parts of his personality? Die with her, in effect?

He wasn't sure at this point.

Fortunately, Rosey *had* been lucky. That stun shot *had* gone wide. She'd survived.

Now, it was up to Dennis to make sure that she continued to live.

Which was why he did *not* approve of Rosey's current plan, namely, to pop out of hyperspace and sail to *Helga*, one of the closest space stations to *Lorenzo*.

"But what if they're waiting for you there?" Dennis pointed out. Again.

Did he deserve such an eyeroll?

No, he did not, thank you very much.

"They won't be," Rosey said. "They won't have anything organized so fast."

Jamaal spoke up at that point. "If we're dealing with Duri—and I assume she's the one coming after you currently—then she probably planned ahead. There might already be operatives just waiting for you to dock there."

"But I need to get back to station command on *Lorenzo*," Rosey complained. "They're already threatening to repossess my workshop space."

"We'll be able to buy it back," Jamaal assured her.

"I doubt it," Rosey said, her tone sounding bitter. "Some developer is going to swoop in and sub-divide the place into four or five apartments. And I'll have to rebuild my workshop from scratch. Plus replacing all my equipment."

"You won't be able to do *any* of that if you're in jail," Dennis helpfully pointed out.

Rosey sighed, frustrated that things weren't going her way.

She wasn't considering how *he* had felt, all that time not being able to access her, to hear her.

To help her.

And how he never wanted to face that again.

"How about this. We come out in the system near *Helga*, but we don't dock with the space station. We should still have communications without tying ourselves down. All right?"

Dennis could tell that Rosey didn't want to take the compromise that Jamaal was offering, but she still agreed grudgingly.

Which was good, because Dennis may, *perhaps*, have been considering changing their course and not popping out there but very far away.

He still took as long as he reasonably could in hyperspace before making the jump back to real space.

No one immediately hailed them. No unfriendly ships nearby

scanned them. No one was *rude*, which Dennis believed to be a good sign.

He dawdled as he brought *The Roadrunner* closer to the station, going slower than Rosey would have. She complained at him, but he didn't really listen to her.

Slow and steady may, indeed, win races now and again.

"Huh," Jamaal said. The Humans were all sitting in the breakfast nook, which was the most comfortable place in the ship, thanks to Dennis's genius.

"Seems the warrant for my arrest has been rescinded," Jamaal said. "Station security would like a chat, but that's about it."

"Does that mean we can go back?" Harkeen asked.

"No. It just means that their first attempt failed. There will be more attempts," Jamaal said grimly.

Ugh.

It occurred to Dennis that not only was he now having to take care of Rosey, but he had to ensure that Jamaal didn't get into more trouble. Because he was sure to drag Rosey down with him.

When had this become his life? When had he started worrying more about people rather than his fabulous décor and upgrades?

"I'm getting messages. A *lot* of messages," Rosey complained. "Station security on *Lorenzo*. Now, station security on *Helga*."

One of the ships attached to the station sent a ping their way.

"Guys, we may have a problem," Dennis said. They were only halfway between the hyperspace area and the station.

The ship that had noticed them had just disconnected from the station.

"What's up?" Rosey said, focusing all her attention on him.

He explained the situation. The other ship hadn't hailed them —they were just headed directly at them.

"We should get back to hyperspace," Jamaal warned.

Dennis fervently agreed.

"Now, hang on," Rosey said. "These idiots aren't going to open fire and try blasting us out of space, not this close to a habitat that they were just connected to."

"No, they'll do much worse than that," Jamaal assured her. "They'll block all electronics on the ship, grab us while we're helpless, then haul us into the station. Or wherever their final destination is."

"Dennis? Can you detect such a field before it hits us?" Rosey said, still stubbornly clinging to the idea that it wasn't as bad as the rest of them believed.

"Affirmative boss," Dennis said grimly. "Electro-magnetic wave field detected and heading our direction."

Dennis had studied some Human body language. The only person he really cared about was Rosey, and so he'd learned to read her better than anyone else.

For a moment—not long in terms of Human measurements of time, but fracking forever in terms of an AI such as himself—Rosey looked unsure.

Scared, even.

Then that stubborn set of her jaw came to the rescue.

"The hell they are," Rosey said, rising from the table and racing up to the helm.

Where she belonged.

It wasn't that much of a fight—*The Roadrunner* didn't have any guns. The other ship never hailed them, nor did it answer any of Rosey's calls.

She did try to get in a call to the station, but the electro-magnetic wave field blocked the signal.

Anyone else in the path of this thing was going to have all their systems knocked out. It was a danger to everyone in the nearby area.

So Rosey didn't try to engage. Didn't lead them on a merry chase. Merely turned and fled, right back into hyperspace.

Such a shame that when the other ship tried to follow them they learned that they weren't fast enough, couldn't even close on them.

For once, Dennis was glad that Rosey kept him so precisely tuned, and had done all those upgrades to his engines.

Dennis barely logged the difference between real space and hyperspace. He was comfortable in all space. Still, he could tell that Rosey, despite her dislike of how hyperspace felt, relaxed.

Rosey sat back in her pilot's chair, her face pensive.

"Dennis? You got any ideas where we should head next?" she asked.

"I do," Dennis purred. He put in the coordinates and Rosey left him to the flying while she went back to take care of her guests.

Places to go. People to see.

And more secrets to uncover.

SIXTEEN

Ajax stood proud before the warlord Constantine, never letting on just how shaken he was.

Over the years, Ajax had seen a lot of gnarly body mods. That techno-wizard Oswald, with spiders crawling out of his shirt and injecting him to keep his system running, had been one of the least gruesome.

It had never occurred to him that someone could go a different direction: instead of focusing on gross improvements to their frame, reaching for Human perfection instead.

Constantine styled himself as a Greek god. Someone whose smile demanded your attention and whose frown required swift obedience. He'd set himself up in a Hellenic mansion outside of the main city on Psykee, with all manner of delightful serving girls and boys in various states of undress. He stood much taller than Ajax, at a little over six foot, four inches tall, and presented an imposing figure. The Greek-style toga he wore was blindingly white, with rich gold details. It made Ajax momentarily feel ashamed of his own bare chest, black vest and black leather pants.

When Constantine's deep, commanding voice instructed Ajax to tell him everything, he found himself stumbling over his words in an effort to please the warlord.

Fortunately, a cynical part of him clung to his disbelief of what was immediately in front of him.

His parents may have been shits (okay, so maybe they were slightly better than shits as they had paid off his ransom to the Kollective) but they'd insisted that if something appeared to be too good to be true, it was.

And Constantine was absolutely too good to be true.

Another thing that Ajax's father had pounded into his head was to never let a con man know that you've seen behind the mask.

So while a part of Ajax kept blubbering and trying to please the warlord, another part of him pulled back, analyzing the situation.

It wasn't good, quite frankly.

He'd had to come to a compromise with Odysseus—Karl "Odysseus" Doukas—the little thief who'd started proclaiming *Hermes 3.0* as his own ship. As Ajax would have been able to beat Odysseus in any sort of physical fight, the worm had immediately capitulated—with terms, though, as he'd apparently paid a couple of guards to stay true to him, and they had kept weapons trained on Ajax during their negotiations. Which had happened in the airlock, right after Ajax had boarded.

Hermes 3.0 was back in Ajax's command. There'd been paperwork that he'd had to sign, labeling Odysseus as his second in command officially and how the worm would inherit the ship in case of Ajax's "untimely" demise.

Ajax didn't ask for any stipulations about not being murdered in his sleep. Any good pirate captain already understood that was a normal hazard and had already taken precautions (as Ajax had, and then tripled when he'd come back on board).

He had talked Odysseus down in terms of his percentage of any profit *Hermes 3.0* might accumulate. A captain had to be perceived of as generous to his men. Being too greedy left not only the men poorer, but the ship as well.

The goons with the guns pointed at him didn't appear to care about that stipulation. Must mean Odysseus was paying them out of his own pockets.

Good to know. Ajax would either buy those men off, or get them killed, sooner or later.

Now, though, with Constantine pulling strings that Ajax had been unaware of, he might have really stepped out of an airlock with minimal air.

He finished telling the warlord about the daring heist of retrieving the alien parts from Oswald, as well as stealing *Aisha* back from him. And how the containers with the original alien artifacts and papers had been retaken as well.

Constantine seemed more amused than angry by the end of Ajax's tale.

"Audacious," he boomed. "Little mice, so clever." Then his mien grew thunderous. "But we can't have mere Humans tweaking the noses of the gods and getting away with it, can we?"

"How can I help?" Ajax said immediately, both the part of him that was still under the spell of the warlord as well as the analytic part understanding that this was the right play.

"I have it on good authority that the princess has left Ishiman and gone back to Niani. There may already be people looking for them," Constantine said with a deadly smile.

"Your people?" Ajax asked. He wanted to understand his role in this upcoming play.

Constantine gave a negligent shrug. "Perhaps," he purred.

Who was already working with Constantine?

Now that Ajax thought about it, much of his story hadn't surprised the warlord. He'd already been informed about what had happened and had already started planning his revenge.

So Constantine had his eyes set on the princess and her lover, Moe.

Great. Hopefully that meant Ajax could focus on Rosey. She was still his enemy, as far as he was concerned. She'd been the one who'd hung him out to dry with the Kollective.

"So, while it might be fun to have you swoop down on *Aisha*, like a hawk on an unsuspecting sparrow, I'd instead like you to be my representative with the space station *Lorenzo*," Constantine said. "It appears that Rosey is in something of a bind with the authorities there. I'd like to purchase her workshop before she returns. Discretely, of course. But then she'll be forced to deal with me."

Ajax nodded. "Smart," he said. "Force her to count her credits." He paused, then gave Constantine a fierce smile of his own. "But what do I get out of it?"

For a moment, surprise flashed across Constantine's face, as if he hadn't expected Ajax to do anything but leap to his bidding.

Then the full force of the Greek god was bearing down on Ajax. "I suppose the satisfaction of a job well done won't be enough, eh?"

Ajax had to clamp his teeth together and force himself not to back down.

"No, it won't be," he managed to grind out.

"Oh, very well," Constantine said, the pressure of his personality lessening a smidgen. With a negligent wave of his hand, he said, "I'll hire you and your crew for this job, then."

That...was unexpected.

Being on the payroll of a warlord like Constantine would bump up his standing with all the rest of the pirates in the system.

He couldn't wait to rub it in their noses.

It did occur to him that Constantine would expect Ajax to accept the contract without reading it or negotiating it.

And though Ajax still considered his parents shits, they had taught him contract law.

He couldn't wait to see Odysseus try to take over after this. Not when Ajax had the backing of Constantine.

Ajax's star may have fallen, but that was a momentary, temporary thing.

It was surely back on the rise, now.

SEVENTEEN

Jun couldn't *believe* her luck.

Here were the papers she needed. She didn't understand all the chemistry involved, but Sano did.

The Atoylee *had* been crafting a chemical weapon up on the moon, away from their planet, so that nothing could accidentally leak and destroy their world.

And all because of the Bukoykan, who Jun would now bet good money had been an alien species who'd been attacking them.

"We have to go," Moe said, running into the room. "An unfriendly ship's found us."

Jun wanted to scream. Maybe even throw herself to the floor and pitch an epic tantrum.

Fortunately, as part of the royal family, she'd trained for emergencies like this. She didn't freeze. She acted.

"Two minutes," she breathed out as she started sorting papers quickly.

They were so delicate! They'd crumble if she treated them harshly. Whatever coating had allowed them to survive in the harshness of vacuum didn't mean they weren't eroding.

She had no choice, though.

She grabbed the ones that she considered most important. Shoved an armful at Moe, who took them without a word.

Sano directed her to grab a few other folders. If Jun could have, she would have grabbed all of them. Maybe even hauled the entire file cabinet.

However, there was a long climb ahead of her. Going up all those stairs, at speed, was going to suck. She couldn't weigh herself down too much. They had to get back up to the surface as quickly as they could.

She nodded at Moe when she was ready. He took off at a run, going back down the hall to the door, waiting for her to join him, then sprinting up the stairs.

No fair! His legs were so much longer than hers. He could go up the stairs two at a time.

"I'm getting back into range with Atilio," Moe suddenly said in her ear, through their comm device. "I'll wait for you there."

Jun let the feeling of his reassurance carry her forward.

And up.

Each flight had sixteen stairs, followed by a landing, a reversal, then another sixteen stairs. Was the number sixteen significant? Was it because they had four hands, and so anything divisible by four was automatically superior? Or was it just architecturally sound?

The railing fascinated her as well.

Human railings had a single handrail on top to slide their hands along.

This railing had two handrails, stacked on top of one another.

Was one for the first set of hands of the Atoylee? And the bottom one for their second set of hands?

Humanity had never found a staircase before. The children's books they'd discovered hadn't had a picture of one, and they'd never found any intact.

And the murals! Why was the top all jungle and natural, while the bottom was geometric, with no actual figures represented? Did that have religious significance? Was it meant to focus the minds of the scientists working there? Plus, while the designs were present in every space that Jun would bet was common, many of the smaller rooms and labs were free from decoration.

Did some find it annoying? Distracting? Or were there pictures or other decorations that had covered those walls once? Maybe even holographic displays, like what Dennis used sometimes?

Jun had so many questions!

Whoever was interrupting them had better have a good accounting of themselves. Because not only was she ready to explode all over them, she was tempted to bring the wrath of the Emperor himself down on their heads.

How had someone found them? She'd only told her parents, her brother Minato, and the spy master Itsuki. He'd been the only one to insist on knowing her location. She'd told the others because she knew they'd worry if she just disappeared. Again.

None of those people would harm her.

She'd been careful not to mention her plans in front of any of the staff. However, had one of those people said something they shouldn't have, in front of someone who carried the story along?

Someone had been trying to kill Minato. The person who'd actually done the poisoning had killed himself while being held, before their questions could be answered.

She didn't necessarily believe that he'd voluntarily taken his own life. Chances were, his hand had been forced. Particularly since the recording from directly outside his cell supposedly had developed a malfunction two weeks beforehand, with no one the wiser. It just seemed far too convenient.

That was, of course, assuming that it was someone from Ishiman who'd come after them. Though Atilio had assured her that he'd found all the tracking bugs from Constantine, *Aisha* may still have had some that were on a delayed timer, that didn't go live until just now.

Too many questions. Again.

Moe was a beacon of light ahead of her, shining down the staircase, lighting her way.

"Moe?" Jun asked as she rested for a moment beside him. "What is Atilio actually worried about?"

She couldn't see his face clearly in his headset, as he turned away from her and started going up the stairs again.

"The guns that were attached to *Aisha* were mis-wired," Moe said grimly. "Deliberately attached wrong."

Jun gasped and started up the stairs again, the desire for the truth pulling her along faster.

"What would happen if we used the guns?" she had to ask as Moe climbed the stairs beside her.

"Atilio said they might have fired once or twice. Then, we would have blown ourselves up," Moe said.

"And he didn't want to tell us anything because he was afraid that I would have reported it, right?" Sano said, speaking on their shared communication channel.

"Yes," Moe said. "I told him that he could trust you. But he wasn't sure of your loyalties. If you could be forced to report, even if you didn't consciously want to."

Sano was quiet for a few moments. "There...were, such circuits installed in me," she admitted.

Jun nodded. "I know. I removed them."

"No, you don't understand," Sano continued. "Itsuki tried to reinstall them while we were on Ishiman, just this last week. Claimed that he needed more access to you, since the attack on your brother. It was to keep you safe."

Sano paused. "I may have consented, then disrupted them once we were in hyperspace, so that I couldn't be forced to give away your location. You did give me that much autonomy," she said, sounding defensive.

"So Itsuki tried to compromise you without my permission?" Jun said, her entire world growing cold.

"He was just looking out for you," Sano assured her.

"But he was also the one who insisted on installing big guns on *Aisha*," Jun said.

"And he may not have known that they'd been wired to blow up," Moe said. "That might have been someone else, some additional plot against the royal family."

Jun nodded and continued plodding up the stairs, deep in thought.

It would pain her to learn that Itsuki had turned against the royal family. He'd been part of their staff forever. She couldn't make any accusation against him unless she had a lot more than coincidence backing her up.

Still, she'd also been trained to consider such things. Her mother had told her that the royal family was only as secure as their staff. If the staff turned against them, they were finished. Which was one of the reasons why the children all had AI governesses, who supposedly couldn't be compromised.

"Sano? Does Minato still have his AI governor?" Jun asked.

"Yes, but he is only a sliver of his former self, barely aware," Sano said, her tone very disapproving. "And Daiki's isn't much better. They don't have the need for such complex computing, not like you with xenolinguistics. Theirs work as servants. Mere assistants."

Jun didn't need for Sano to continue, the unspoken words clear between them.

Her brothers' AIs weren't partners, which was what Sano truly was to her.

"Do you think they've been compromised?" Jun said.

"How would they be compromised? Their basic programming is to protect their charge. The entire construct would have to be rewritten from scratch to get around that," Sano said.

"Was Atilio right to be worried?" Moe said after a couple more flights.

"No," Sano said quietly. "I would never put Jun at risk. And granting a third party some sort of tracking capability of my charge would be just that."

"Because I did give Sano that much autonomy," Jun said, trying to reassure Moe.

She wasn't sure if Moe was reassured at all. Or if Moe was even the one she needed to talk with. No, she needed to have a nice, long, oh-so-comfy chat with Atilio about this.

Swell.

In the meanwhile, they had to get back to the surface. Atilio wasn't responding to their comm messages, which meant that he'd had to fly off with *Aisha*, to try to lure away whoever was out there.

Because they were all in trouble if the other ship landed a crew on the moon. While Jun knew that Moe would do his best to protect her, Atilio would be the one to shoot first and ask questions never.

So they climbed. And they listened to their own panting breaths.

But Atilio remained silent.

———

Jun's legs felt wobbly, and not just because no one was waiting for them in the little elevator room on the surface. Atilio hadn't come back, but he had told Moe that he'd leave a message for them on the flitter if he had to run.

Moe stalked forward with his stunner out, ready to defend them.

No one showed up, though, not in the corridor leading out. They paused in the doorway that led to the surface, looking up. Sano used the optics on Jun's EVA suit but couldn't discern any ships above them.

They darted out and bounded from the opening to the flitter. It surprised Jun how well Moe worked in such low gravity. Then again, he'd probably practiced at it.

Once they were on the flitter, Jun took off her helmet as soon as Sano gave the all clear, though she didn't bother taking off her suit. She carefully put down the papers she'd been carrying on a table that Moe folded down from the wall. Then she followed Moe into the cockpit.

The flitter was only about twelve meters long, with a cockpit at one end and a storage hold at the other, while the engines took up space on top of the ship. It had been the flitter that had originally taken the alien artifacts and papers from Niani, so many weeks ago.

A recording from Atilio waited for them there.

"Ha ha! Sucker!" he started off with.

Jun startled at the vehemence in his voice.

"I was just waiting for you and that bitch to leave the ship. Never thought I'd double-cross you, eh, boss?" Atilio continued.

Jun felt all the blood drain out of her face.

"Constantine offered me a really sweet deal for *Aisha*, though. I'm thinking I'll take him up on it, since you'll never amount to anything," Atilio sneered.

Though Jun knew that the air in the flitter was fine, it felt as though it had all been sucked out of the room.

"Good luck catching up with me. Even if you went around the Shilane moon twice in a slingshot maneuver, you'd never match my speed. See ya—never!"

That was an odd thing to say. Wasn't it?

Moe merely nodded, though.

The message started to repeat itself. Moe listened a second time, his face serious. But it was just repeat, nothing different between the two versions.

He turned it off, then looked at Jun, his face morose.

"What do we do?" Jun asked gently. She didn't want to think about how much pain Moe must be in, with his best friend turning on him that way.

"Now, we wait," Moe said.

He cracked a big grin.

"What?" Jun asked, questioning his expression as much as anything. Had the pressure just gotten to him?

"Atilio was probably afraid that who ever was out there was listening in. So he came up with a performance for them, to throw them off track," Moe said.

"Oh. Oh!" Jun said, surprised.

Maybe that had been the case. But had he really needed to call her such things?

"Talking about Constantine let me know that Atilio suspected the other craft was one of his," Moe continued. "That time reference? Tells me he'll be back in two hours. However, since he sent it forty-five minutes ago, we probably only have to wait an hour and fifteen minutes."

"You're sure he'll be back?" Jun said, still shaken at how good of a "performance" Atilio had put on.

"I am," Moe assured her. He sat down at the controls of the flitter and started a search of the skies above them.

No ship registered.

Moe set up an automated alarm, so that when a ship did come into range, the flitter would notify them.

"All right," Jun said, calculating how much she could do in seventy-five minutes. "I'm exhausted and I need to rest. I also need to make sure I have good scans of all of the papers we've accumulated so far, as this environment might cause them to decay faster, and I don't have any sort of preservation unit to put them into."

She paused, spearing Moe with a glare. "Once Atilio gets back, if we don't have to race away from this system, I'm going back down and getting more data."

"Got it," Moe said. "Can I help?"

Jun knew that Sano was all the help she needed.

Still, she wouldn't turn down his company.

"Sure," she said, walking back to the airlock where the papers had been temporarily set.

When the flitter alarm announced that a ship was above them, Jun and Moe shared a frown.

That was far too soon for Atilio. It had only been thirty minutes or so.

Who had found them now?

EIGHTEEN

Atilio cursed at those idiots following him once again.

It was good that Rosey had spent some time tuning *Aisha*'s systems. She wasn't as fast as *The Roadrunner*—it would take another full upgrade for the engines to even start approaching the other ship's speed.

However, *Aisha* was still not as fast as Atilio would like.

As those assholes behind him were proving.

The other ship had been silent on its initial approach. Was it trying to see how long it took for *Aisha* to respond? To get a better gauge of the ship's sensor range?

Atilio waited as long as he felt comfortable before he finally tried hailing them.

He'd been expecting pirates. Some jumped-up punks too hot under the collar to negotiate in a reasonable fashion.

Not a lackadaisical ship's captain informing him that they were a repossession crew and were there to take *Aisha* back to the bank.

Atilio knew, *knew*, that Moe had made all his payments on time.

Somehow, Constantine had gotten to the bank and convinced

them to call in the loan immediately instead of the decade or so that Moe had left to pay off his debt.

Atilio ran the configuration of the other ship through the computers, getting an answer he didn't like.

It really was a repo ship. Was it in Constantine's pay, or had the bank hired them?

Either way, he couldn't take a chance on letting them get too close. A repo ship wouldn't just have an electro-magnetic wave field generator, they'd have beams and other toys they could use to scoop up an errant piece of property.

He quickly left a decoy message for Moe, cringing at the term he used for the princess but desperate to put anyone listening off the scent, in case the repo ship had additional "business" out here.

Then he raced away, trying to put as much distance as he could between him and the other ship.

It was good that *Aisha* was fast.

However, the other ship was faster. Not by much. It was taking them a while to close on *Aiasha* again.

Atilio didn't want to jump into hyperspace, but he felt as though he didn't have a choice. It was the only way to escape the ship hunting him. Hopefully, he'd make it back to the moon in the timeline he'd given Moe.

He took a deep breath as soon as the world slightly shifted. It didn't really matter where he jumped to. He wasn't aware of any technology that allowed ships to be tracked through hyperspace.

The jump was less than ten minutes. Enough to put him in the next system. He deliberately came out in a place that as far as he knew was uninhabited. (Didn't mean it necessarily was. Space was big, and Humans had a reputation for wanting to get away from everything and everyone.)

Atilio was all set to jump back to Lawaka when *Aisha* let him know that another ship had entered the system.

It was the repo ship.

How in all the hells had it found him?

"*Aisha*," the other captain said on the comm. "This is your last warning. Any additional jumps into hyperspace will result in severe monetary penalties. Let us approach."

That told Atilio two things.

One, that somehow the repo ship *could* follow him. There had to be some sort of sophisticated tracking equipment on *Aisha* that Atilio wasn't aware of.

Two, the repo ship probably was actually from the bank. No one but a creditor would hound him so hard.

He couldn't fire on the repo ship. Not without risking blowing himself up. Plus, a quick scan confirmed that they had much larger guns that probably did work. Possibly they weren't well used, because the bank would want its property back, not scraps.

Aisha raced to the far end of the current system, the repo ship gaining on them all the while as Atilio ran through the ship, using Rosey's tracker on every surface, looking for the tracker that the bank was using.

It wasn't until he was back on the bridge that he realized what he was looking for was staring him in the face.

The merchant's clock. It kept time as it was counted on the bank's planet, a constant reminder of the amount of money that Moe owed.

The bank had installed it. Moe had maintained it and kept it running, no matter what else around them broke.

Atilio had never really looked at it. He'd certainly never touched it or removed the shielding around it. Ugly red warning signs and promises of penalties were etched into the metal.

Still, it was the only thing that made sense.

However, Atilio wasn't about to work on something as delicate as the merchant's clock while he was in hyperspace. The dark outlines of all surfaces meant doing electrical work blind, only able to feel the wires.

So he had to jump again.

While he was in hyperspace, he gathered every conceivable tool he might need, and several that he probably wouldn't but grabbed just in case, placing them in precise rows in front of the console.

As soon as he came out of hyperspace, he started trying to back out the screws holding the merchant's clock into the control panel.

Of course they'd use a custom size.

And just to mess with anyone trying to do the very stupid thing that Atilio was attempting, they didn't use the same custom size on each of the corners. No, two were bigger.

Atilio ground his teeth and worked as quickly as he could, red-necking together a bastard of a screwdriver/socket wrench to get the first four bolts out.

Then he had to run again as the repo ship had arrived, giving him all sorts of dire warnings. He set *Aisha* on a zig-zagging course across the system he was currently in as he kept working.

At least the repo captain wasn't threatening him with violence.

Yet.

It took three more jumps before Atilio managed to get the cover off.

At least the wiring underneath was fairly straight-forward.

Atilio disconnected all but the power supply to the clock before he took the final jump into hyperspace.

He didn't want to disappear off the repo's sensors while they were still in system. They'd know what he did.

If he just disappeared in hyperspace and they couldn't find him again, well, that meant they kept searching until they decided he'd done something stupid and blown himself up.

That was when Atilio discovered the next problem.

As soon as he jumped into hyperspace, additional wires appeared connecting the merchant's clock to the control panel. At least a dozen more.

Atilio swore. Loudly. Cursing the inventors of such a thing with both plagues and uncomfortable body positions.

However, it made sense, now that he was looking at it.

Hyperspace always put such hard edges on things.

Why not use wire that was practically invisible in normal space when connecting up a piece of equipment that shouldn't be disturbed? If Atilio hadn't been in such desperate need, he never would have stumbled across them. Possibly the clock would have appeared broken and Atilio wouldn't have known any better until the repo ship came back into range.

It took Atilio longer to figure out this wiring because he was effectively working blind. He couldn't see the wire color, didn't know which wires were hot and which weren't. Instead of just reaching for a wire, he always had to test it.

Had whoever had invented this security system also created a new set of lenses that Humans could wear to see through the hyperspace lines? Or was there some sort of robot who did this work?

Atilio couldn't wait to tell Rosey about it. She was the only one he knew who would appreciate the deviousness of this design.

And who might possibly want to figure out how to use it for herself.

Finally, Atilio disconnected all the wires, never once shocking himself into unconsciousness though he did zing his fingers a couple of times. He'd had to reset *Aisha*'s course three times, extending how far he was jumping.

Atilio allowed the ship to come back into normal space.

Then, he waited.

After an hour had passed, he finally felt assured that the repo ship wasn't going to be finding him anytime soon.

He was certain that some sort of ITT had been inserted into the metal of the clock's shielding. He was either going to have to space the entire clock, or figure out a faraday cage that would block the tag.

In the meantime, he was late.

Hopefully Jun and Moe would forgive him for his tardiness.

NINETEEN

Jamaal had a bad feeling when Moe told them about the unfriendly ship that had appeared in the system while they'd been deep in the base, unable to communicate with Atilio.

Jun explained it away, saying that she hadn't been secretive about where they were planning on traveling to. Any sort of chance conversation might have sparked their stalker.

Jamaal's gut said otherwise. He'd been an operative for too long. This sort of "coincidence" was anything but. Again, he had to wonder if his old handler had anything to do with this, if she knew what was going on.

No one wanted to leave the system until Atilio returned. Rosey was the only one of them who appeared unconcerned when he missed his return window, assuring them that he was just off hot-dogging it around the system somewhere.

Jun took Rosey's word for it, and insisted on descending back to the base. There was work to do.

As *The Roadrunner* came equipped with a couple of EVA suits, that meant Jamaal and Harkeen could go with Jun and Moe. Rosey had agreed to remain with *The Roadrunner*, knowing that she could outrun anything that showed up, and was the one best equipped to do so.

Thus, Jamaal found himself looking around with wonder at the base of the Atoylee. He'd heard rumors of such a moon base before—the other alien hunters had of course discerned that there might be something there.

Reading about the possibility was one thing.

Actually walking through it was something else.

As they'd descended, Jamaal had gladly listened to Jun rattling away with theories as to why the living spaces were so different than the communal spaces in terms of decoration, why the upper floor had living pictures portrayed, why the base itself hadn't decayed more.

Now, she was off gathering papers together (though she'd been at pains to explain that it wasn't paper, not exactly, as that would have long since been destroyed). Jamaal and Harkeen took their time poking their noses into the various rooms, taking careful samples of cloth and furniture that was already falling into dust.

A comm request came on—Harkeen wanting to talk with Jamaal on a private channel.

"On a scale of one to ten, how excited are you right now?" Harkeen purred into his ear.

"Four," Jamaal shot back immediately. "Maybe a five."

"Liar," Harkeen chuckled.

All right. So maybe Harkeen had a point.

While Jamaal had always been focused on finding living aliens, being able to explore an alien base that hadn't been destroyed *was* exciting.

"Maybe an eight," Jamaal admitted.

"I knew it. So, do I have to punish you later for lying? Or reward you for telling the truth?" Harkeen teased.

"Both?" Jamaal said enthusiastically.

"Both it is," Harkeen promised.

Jamaal found himself grinning.

He'd originally brought Harkeen along to help remind him of his softer side, so he wouldn't get too serious or go down old, well-trodden paths that led to killing people.

Instead, they'd been finding each other. Harkeen had a passionate side that this trip had really brought to the forefront. Jamaal had had no complaints about their lovemaking before this, but there was an intensity there now that had been missing.

Perhaps it was the ever-present sense of danger, that this might be their last time together.

"How excited are you?" Jamaal asked as he used a spoon to gather together some of the dust on what he assumed was a bed, then slide it carefully into a sealable plastic bag. (Jun had bemoaned their lack of actual equipment, but they did what they could.) The fibers had all dissolved, but the pattern they'd made had maintained, a geometric quilt made out of ashes.

"At being here? Or the prospect of what we're going to be doing later on?" Harkeen replied.

"Both," Jamaal said, laughing at how he'd repeated himself.

Harkeen paused, collecting his thoughts.

That was one of the things that Jamaal liked (loved? Was there love there?) about the other man—he wouldn't just fly off the handle when it came to anything. He frequently stopped and thought before he spoke. Some might find that annoying, but Jamaal had come to appreciate the force of the other man's intellect and emotional intelligence.

"Like you, I'm probably only at a six or seven for being here. It's cool and all, don't get me wrong. But aliens have never been my thing. You know?" Harkeen said.

Jamaal nodded, even though Harkeen couldn't see it. They had different passions. However, they also had enough commonality that they never seemed to run out of things to talk about, such as music, art, and cooking.

"As for what we'll be doing later, well, that's probably already a twelve," Harkeen said.

That was the other thing. Harkeen wasn't afraid to admit to his feelings, whether sexual or emotional. That sort of bravery was different than what Jamaal was used to. Particularly since he'd had to hide his true self away for so many years.

Earlier, they'd found another door, one without a door handle, hidden among the geometric designs. Jamaal had used the decoder that Moe and Jun had cobbled together (though honestly, he was going to have to improve it) to power the lock on the door, and managed to it slide open.

Inside had been a smallish room, filled with crumbling equipment. The radioactive substance used to power the machine was still radiating, though the door and the walls around it had completely shielded it.

So the Atoylee had had some level of nuclear power. It was probably why the base was still in such good condition: the equipment wouldn't have stopped working until something broke.

Rosey was going to want to get down here at some point and see the machine for herself.

Moe had come down with them again, and was making regular trips up and down the stairs to stay in contact with Rosey and the ship. However, they didn't have an endless air supply, and it would take time to go to the ship.

At least Jamaal was in good enough shape that he hadn't felt like he was dying after coming down them. Going back up might be another matter.

Unless Harkeen made it a race.

Then Jamaal would never admit to how tired he was. Even if it meant time with Harkeen gently massaging his legs.

Wait, why was he going to deny anything? If that would be the result?

"Good news!" came Moe's excited voice over the shared comm channel. "Atilio has returned."

"Are we heading back up?" Jamaal said, feeling himself come to attention, his body already ready for action.

"Aye. Jun, how much longer do you need?" Moe asked.

"Three months? Maybe four?" she teased. Then she gave enough of a heavy sigh that Jamaal could feel her frustration across the distance. "Fine. Five minutes. I'll need help carrying papers up."

"You got it," Jamaal said, looking around the little apartment he stood in.

He tried to imagine it as it had been. Thick carpet. Colorful quilt on the bed, maybe a changing mosaic displayed on the wall, something that even Dennis may have approved of. Desk in the corner, though that had already collapsed, as had the chair.

A cold place now, but it had probably been warm and full of life at one point.

Jamaal took a few more samples then went to join the others, gathering up his allotment of papers to carry to the surface.

As exciting as it was to see an alien ruin intact, this place was still dead.

And Jamaal was very much focused on not just living aliens, but on living, himself.

TWENTY

Duri smirked when the report about the bank's repo of *Aisha* came to her desk. It was later in the afternoon, the sun casting long shadows across the government building on New Rome. She'd already finished her tea and was debating either getting Kiley to make more or going home early.

The report caused her to order tea.

It appeared that Rosey and Jamaal's new acquaintance had someone coming after them.

Using the bank had been a brilliant move. Duri wished she would have thought of that herself.

She was going to have to remember it as a tactic the next time she needed to apply pressure to someone as broke as Moe.

The question was, though, *who* had gotten to the bank?

While the warlord Constantine imagined himself as some sort of Greek god, she doubted that he had that long of a reach. Or that he would have considered such a ploy. Duri did have the entire story of what had occurred from the littlest pirate while he'd been under her control, how Rosey *et al* had stolen from the warlord. However, Duri had no corroboration that the events had occurred as Ajax had told them.

Having the bank repo *Aisha* as a way of getting it back under

Constantine's control seemed too indirect for him. No, he'd send his goons out to get the ship back.

Who had contacted the bank?

And could she find them? Seek them out to make common cause with them?

Duri set the military research team that ostensibly reported to her to the task of ferreting out who'd tipped the hand of the bank.

The answer came back surprisingly early the next morning, and it was more layered than she would have expected.

It probably *had* been Constantine who'd contacted the bank. They didn't have proof of it, of course. However, he had made a large deposit to that particular bank that was just this side of being legal. Probably other money had also changed hands, none of it traceable.

While Constantine had his credits secured in multiple financial institutions (and schemes that Duri wasn't about to waste her time taking apart), he'd never done a deal with this particular bank before. Sure, it was in Allied Worlds space, but a pretty good distance from Constantine's usual circles.

What was more interesting was that Constatine probably hadn't come up with all that money himself.

No, a large chunk of cash had landed in Constantine's pockets days before he'd made contact with the bank.

And Duri's team couldn't figure out where it had come from.

Track the money was always good advice. The military research team had tracked the credits trickling into Constantine's accounts with a fair amount of accuracy. It hadn't arrived in one massive chunk, no, it had come in through multiple avenues over the course of three days. The amounts, though, of Constantine's deposit to the bank and the credits deposited into his accounts had been the exact same.

Where this money had come from was another matter.

There were miss-wires, money that had been deposited, pulled back, then re-deposited, though with a different amount, the numbers reversed, like seven hundred sixty-two the first time and seven hundred twenty-six the second. The accounts that the money had been transferred from were all newly created, within the past week. Each transfer had been insignificant, not enough to alert any of the automated tracking systems. It was only by chance that one of the researchers had even found a pattern.

Only someone who was a master of their craft and confident in their assets could afford this sort of shell game.

But who?

Duri knew that someone had tried to kill Prince Minato. The killer had been caught red-handed by the Imperial guard.

Yet, that killer had been allowed to commit suicide, the recording equipment mysteriously not working, having not worked for a couple of weeks, a glitch that no one had caught beforehand.

Were the two events connected? The attempt on the prince's life, and now these money transfers? Was someone actually after the damned princess and not the poor ship captain? Though, according to Ajax, that was one and the same, as the two had been insufferably gooey-eyed at each other the entire time he'd been there.

Duri kept some of her researchers tracking the money, seeing what else they could learn, if they could find whoever was behind this. It would be good to find another ally, particularly one who appeared to have such a long, shadowy reach. She let the rest continue their search for Rosey and Jamaal.

Of course, when she found whoever was using Constantine, if they were as smart as they appeared, they wouldn't threaten her. And she wouldn't threaten them. She just wanted to aid them in their quest to completely ruin all of the lives of those involved.

Particularly Rosey and Jamaal.

But where were those two? She hadn't had another report since that idiot had gone after them at space station *Helga*. They'd jumped long this last time, she'd bet.

Anyone who went up against *The Roadrunner* couldn't count on being faster than that ship. And the idiots who'd been trying to collect them should have figured that out themselves. She shouldn't have to point it out to them. *Of course* Rosey had rebuilt the engines on her ship. The original specs couldn't be counted on.

Duri sat and thought as she sipped her tea, considering her conversation earlier with Kiley and where Rosey might jump to.

It was such a big universe. Both Rosey and Jamaal had contacts across all of the three hundred worlds.

Chasing them was probably moot at this point.

So Duri turned her attention back to the princess and Moe.

Where had the repo ship found *Aisha*?

Niani. Of course.

Did something connect the dead aliens with the live ones?

Duri gasped out loud, a move that would never do. Security listening devices were still attached to the underside of her desk. Such a gasp would have been recorded.

And pondered.

She tried to cover it with a cough and banging her tea mug down wincingly hard on her desk.

Maybe they wouldn't know that she'd been shocked. Maybe she could lead them to believe that she'd just swallowed her tea wrong.

However, now that she was considering it, there *had* to be some connection between the two alien species. Why else would this Princess Jun go back to the dig? Why had that been so important? Particularly when she had artifacts from living aliens in her hands?

Had the dead race been in contact with the living aliens?

And should Duri send a team there?

Both of the planets that had at one point had alien species on them were considered "neutral" space. Not just one government oversaw them, even though Niani was in the Empire's space and Zonami was in Kollective space. No, information about the past aliens was too important to be bound by petty political fences.

Even Duri in her obsession for finding living aliens understood that.

Though of course, it would be best if the Kollective found the living aliens first, so they could get the right impression of what Humanity was all about. Order and law, not chaos and inherited, corrupt power.

So while technically, Duri could send any team she'd like to Niani, in reality, it would be best if she had some reason for being there, something that she could easily detail in a report to her superiors.

A connection between the living and dead alien races was just speculation at this point.

Still, all the papers about the dig that the princess had been participating in (and had secretly funded) were slowly being released to scholars.

Maybe there was something in those that Duri could find.

She had Kiley arrange a meeting with the head of her research team, starting in an hour. Maybe she'd divide them up, keep just a few looking for Rosey and Jamaal while the rest worked on deciphering the Niani artifacts.

In the meantime, Duri started pulling down all the papers that had been translated and released, as well as the originals, so she could just hand them to her team and tell them to go.

Something was there.

She just had to find it.

TWENTY-ONE

Rosey oohed and ahhed over the pictures that Dennis displayed of the alien base, as was expected of her. She sat with Atilio in the breakfast nook, sipping her peppermint tea while Atilio had some sludge that he claimed was coffee. They were waiting for the rest of the crew to climb back up the stairs and join them.

Hopefully, Atilio had given that repo ship the slip. At least for the time being.

She was glad that Atilio had made it back alive and well. Moreso than she would have imagined. He'd really started to grow on her.

Possibly like some sort of fungus.

However, he wouldn't be there for long. Moe would go off on his own, and Atilio would follow him.

And Rosey would be by herself. As always.

"You know, I've never thought about doing strict geometric designs before!" Dennis told her as he finished the recording.

"Maybe in the hallway leading to engineering?" Rosey mused.

"That's a thought," Atilio said. "To help focus the mind."

"Exactly!" Dennis said. "When are we going to a station? So I can put in the order for this work?"

Rosey grimaced, unhappy about the reminder that she still had warrants out for her arrest. "When we can," she said.

"Oh. Sorry. Right," Dennis said. "I'll start with reprogramming some of the usual holographic displays. Just to get all the colors right."

"You do that," Rosey said dryly.

Then she turned to Atilio. "You want to set up some experiments with the hyperspace wiring?"

"I would love to," he said, "but first, we need to take a look at the wiring on *Aisha*."

"Got it," Rosey said. She was personally affronted that someone would mis-wire something like a gun, part of the ship's protection. "How long will that take?"

"I don't know," Atilio said, giving his own grimace. "I didn't want to touch it until I had someone looking over my shoulder. I don't know if there's some sort of boobytrap included, something I need to be careful of while I'm doing the work."

"All right," Rosey said. She checked the clock.

It would still take the group another thirty minutes to make it to the surface, then they had to fly back up to *The Roadrunner*.

"Let's go take a preliminary look," she suggested. "We won't do any work until after we see what was done, and have figured out how to undo it."

"Roger that," Atilio said, looking relieved. "Thank you for your help."

"You got it," Rosey said.

The smile he gave her made her wonder.

Was he just appreciative of her expertise?

Or was there something more going on?

***

As far as Rosey could tell—and Dennis concurred—the mis-wiring of the guns wouldn't be that difficult to fix. She didn't see any sort of boobytrap, though they'd be doing a lot of wire tracing to make sure of that, once they started the work.

By the time they'd finished their inspection and come up with some preliminary plans, everyone had joined them in *The Roadrunner*, flying up from the surface.

Dennis and Sano had instructed Rosey on hacking together a storage unit to help preserve the papers that Jun was carrying up. All the samples that Jamaal and Harkeen had collected were also placed in the ugly, black box.

It wasn't that Rosey had an aversion to black. However, the 3D printer that she had on *The Roadrunner* for creating small mechanical parts had been running low on base chemicals (something she'd been meaning to order more of and had forgotten) so black had been the only color she had an abundance of.

For some reason, her favorite rosy color was almost all used up. As was the shiny silver.

For now, it would have to do.

"So, what next?" Rosey asked as the group reconvened for dinner that night.

"I'd like to stay here for a few more days," Jun said immediately. "Gather more samples."

Jamaal shook his head, the serious side of his persona rising. "I don't think that's smart. The repo ship will come back here sooner or later. Plus, we don't know who else will show up. We should leave here, at least for a while."

"And go where?" Moe asked softly. "I feel as though we're kind of a sitting duck, no matter where we go."

Rosey nodded. The usually morose pilot had a point.

"I have an idea," Sano said, quietly joining the conversation.

"Okay," Rosey said, nodding. She wondered when the AIs might have a breakthrough.

"I've been scanning the papers left by the Atoylee," she said. "And I—"

"Along with me," Dennis interrupted.

"We," Sano said, correcting herself, "have been using the three sets of space coordinates to try to interpret where the original alien wreck may have come from. Where it had jumped from, before it landed in our space."

"Ohhh," Jamaal said.

"Smart," Atilio commented.

Rosey merely nodded.

"We have a set of potential destinations," Sano continued. "If we're not going to stay here, I think exploring these possible locations could be fruitful."

"Absolutely," Jamaal said, agreeing at once.

"Really?" Harkeen said, rolling his eyes at Jamaal's enthusiasm, but at the same time, reaching out and quickly squeezing his hand.

Jamaal didn't blush, or at least Rosey didn't think he did, not with that dark skin of his. He still seemed slightly embarrassed by the teasing.

Rosey was so happy for her friend. She hoped that Jamaal could see what he had, and that he would continue to value it, even after they got back and were living in more normal circumstances.

"While I would love to continue collecting samples from the base," Jun said slowly, "I also think taking some time to analyze and digest what we have wouldn't be the worst thing in the world. As much as it pains me to leave here without gathering up absolutely everything."

Rosey understood. Jun had explained that chances were, everything that remained in the base would continue to disintegrate quickly at this point. She had managed to grab most, if not all, of the papers that she'd found, putting them into backpacks the second group had worn so they could carry more.

"I'd like to go with you," Moe said. "In *Aisha*."

"Of course!" Rosey proclaimed. "We wouldn't think of leaving you behind. Besides, there are still things that need to be fixed on your ship."

That earned her an eyeroll from Atilio.

What, just because Rosey hated to leave a project half-done? It wasn't just so that she could spend more time with Atilio. Really.

"All right, then we're decided," Dennis announced. "Sano and I will coordinate between the two ships and get us on our way."

The group broke up soon after that, and in less than an hour, they had left the system and were headed toward the first location.

Rosey slept while they flew, that being one of the few things that she found comfortable to do while in hyperspace. She let Dennis handle the particulars, coordinating with *Aisha* on the series of jumps that would take them far beyond Allied Worlds' space.

And hopefully end up someplace interesting.

———

The first three places where they popped out of hyperspace were a bust. Dead systems with no signs of life, no wrecked ships, nothing.

Rosey hadn't given up hope. Jamaal's enthusiasm helped.

Then they reached the fourth location.

A gas giant floated near them, with colorful storms blowing across its surface. The ring of debris flying around the planet was fairly narrow. Either the asteroids were getting caught and sliding down toward the surface, or whatever had been destroyed in the first place hadn't been that big.

"Got it!" Dennis announced almost immediately after they'd arrived.

"Got what?" Rosey asked, startled and wary.

"Metal confirmed," Sano's voice said. "Either that's an asteroid composed of the exact same metal signatures as the first alien wreck, or there's an alien ship here."

Rosey's heart started beating quickly, familiar adrenaline racing through her system.

Had they actually found another wreck? Or would it be less destroyed, and more of a ship, that she could examine?

It took about twenty minutes to reach their destination. Dennis converted every display that usually put up pictures on the walls to showing the artifact they were approaching.

Though Rosey wouldn't know for certain until after she'd had a chance to do a more significant search of the craft, she would bet that it was identical to the first wreck that she'd examined.

Ha! She'd been right. The front cone of the ship was painted red.

She should have bet Dennis about that, earned herself a few credits, instead of listening to his abuse.

This ship, while probably non-functional, was much more intact than the first one had been. It hadn't been shredded by hyperspace. Short stubby wings extended from the body. Rosey assumed that the four round tubes mounted on them were guns of some sort. Additional guns stuck out from either side of the nose.

The top of the ship had been blown off. Rosey doubted they'd find a body inside. Maybe it had drifted away and was nearby. She shuddered at the thought of someone, anyone, dying in space like that.

A rounded curve made up the tail of the craft. Had something else been there, and blown off? Maybe. Rosey would have to get closer to see what sort of damage the ship had incurred.

"Dennis, prep the holding bays. We're going to take a flitter, snag that craft, and bring it back here," Rosey instructed.

Dennis actually sputtered. "What if it's contaminated? Some sort of alien tech that will eat through my systems? Are you sure this is safe?"

Rosey rolled her eyes. "It's been sitting in vacuum for a while. Any bugs will be long dead."

"But there might be nanobots—or something!—that will attack once they've warmed up!" Dennis complained.

After a deep sigh, Rosey replied. "You can scan the ship to your heart's content, both before and after we bring it in. Just to make sure it's safe."

"Can I blast it with disinfectant?" Dennis asked hopefully.

"No, because we don't want to accidentally damage any plastic wiring," Rosey said. "Just set the holding bay up as a clean room, okay?"

"Fine," Dennis grumbled. "But if it starts eating away at my deck until there's nothing left, I get to say, 'I told you so'."

"Got it," Rosey said.

She glanced over at Jamaal, whose eyes were bigger than an anime character.

She wasn't about to tease him, though.

Here was proof, another actual alien ship, from a recently living culture.

Hopefully not one intent on blowing itself up.

<h1 style="text-align:center">TWENTY-TWO</h1>

Moe didn't have a lot to do at this point.

Jun and Sano were busy with the alien ship, deciphering everything they could. The new ship had also had a data recorder, similar to the first one. It had contained a lot more information that they were gleefully combing through.

Atilio and Rosey were crawling all over the alien ship, doing analysis of the metal, the wiring, the fabric from the pilot's seat that hadn't yet disintegrated, the control panel that was still mostly intact, trying to wring every bit of information they could from the ship in terms of its manufacture.

At least they had taken an afternoon and fixed *Aisha*'s guns. He hoped he'd never have to use them, but it was good that at least he had the option now.

Jamaal moved between the two teams, taking notes, coordinating, making sure that any discoveries by one group was instantly shared with the other. He was like a kid in a candy store, with a large chunk of credits and unable to figure out what to buy.

Luckily, Moe wasn't the only one on the sidelines. Harkeen, also, watched from the edges.

Moe figured that out the first day, when they'd both arrived in the kitchen aboard *The Roadrunner* at the same time, with the intent to fix dinner for everyone else.

Moe was a good enough cook, able to make tasty food from the canned stores that he carried.

Harkeen, though, was an inspired cook, who could make those same ingredients sing.

After that first meal, Moe had brought all the spices he carried over to *The Roadrunner* and the pair of them had taken over cooking for everyone else, preparing meals in the morning and the evening, with just a pick-me-up snack midday. That gave them an excuse to interrupt the others and make them take a break.

Moe and Harkeen had gotten to know each other, and had found each other's strengths and weaknesses when it came to cooking. Moe was really good with spices, and always knew exactly what to pair together, usually based on dishes that he'd grown up eating. While Harkeen was also an excellent cook, he came up with unusual flavor combinations, experimenting more than Moe ever did. In addition, Harkeen could bake and was teaching Moe some of his bread recipes.

That afternoon, while the rustic garlic-and-beer loaf was rising, they sat together in the breakfast nook, sipping their respective drinks and chatting. (Moe had a delightful chai tea with just enough black pepper in it to make it zingy, while Harkeen drank coffee that was possibly spiked with some brandy.)

"So where did you meet Jamaal?" Moe said, finally asking the question that he'd had for a week or more now.

"Dancing, actually," Harkeen replied, his rich laugh filling the quiet nook. "You know that I run a gallery and event space, right?"

Moe nodded. Harkeen had mentioned it before. It meant that he had much more wealth than Moe had ever accumulated. Though if he continued working for Jun and the Emperor's royal family, well, he, too, might eventually have some money.

Though he was going to pay back his loan from the bank.

Atilio might have removed the merchant's clock, but Moe still felt an obligation to zero out his debt.

He didn't want to become *that guy*.

"So we were having a pretty big party one night, with a DJ I actually liked, who played dance music, not the stuff you just shuffle your feet to, or that's so discordant you have a headache after listening for an hour," Harkeen said. "In walked this flamboyant merchant, in his orange robes, looking like he always carried a party with him, stashed away someplace." Harkeen paused, smiling at the memory. "I asked him to dance."

"And that was that?" Moe said. He didn't suggest love at first sight. These two were still dancing around each other, still finding their steps.

"Sort of," Harkeen said. "Jamaal had a lot going on in those days. We had coffee a few times, went out to dinner. We were a thing pretty much from the get-go, but we weren't exclusive. Particularly since Jamaal was traveling a lot."

Moe felt as though there was something else that Harkeen wasn't saying, something about the work that Jamaal had been doing.

No one had mentioned to Moe that Jamaal might have at one point been a spy or something along those lines for the Emperor. Moe hadn't seen that potential until he'd started spending a lot of time with Jamaal. Some of the actions that Jamaal took reminded Moe of Atilio, who'd been in the military. Jamaal cultivated an easy-going, lackadaisical nature—until something needed doing, and then he turned hard and cold. Atilio got so focused that Moe had a hard time breaking him out of wherever his head had taken him.

Moe would bet that Atilio had been out from the service for longer than Jamaal. Or that he hadn't been in as deeply. Or perhaps both.

However, it wasn't Moe's place to ask. Jamaal would tell him about it of his own accord. Or he wouldn't.

"It's only been the last year or so that Jamaal has really let me get close," Harkeen said, with a nod and a soft smile. "I plan on sticking right here, too."

"I'm sure he'll appreciate that," Moe assured Harkeen.

The other man just shrugged and shook his head. "Hopefully. Or I may have to beat some sense into him. We'll see."

Moe just chuckled.

"How did you and Atilio meet?" Harkeen asked.

Moe grimaced. That wasn't as comfortable a story. Still, he wasn't ashamed of his past. He'd worked hard to not become *that guy*.

And had mostly succeeded.

"I'd made a couple of bad business ventures," Moe admitted. More than two, actually. "Normally, I have a well-developed system for selecting goods from one planetary system that are valuable in another. I had a string of bad luck, though. I didn't have the credits to keep paying my crew, so I had to let them all go."

Moe shook his head. Those had been some pretty bleak times, when he'd seriously debating having to sell *Aisha* just to keep food in his own belly.

"Then I ran across a deal that I *knew* would turn a profit. A good one." And it had. Mostly. There had been some fees involved that had halved his gross, so he hadn't made the profit that he'd needed. "I couldn't run *Aisha* by myself. Not with the engines as they'd been. So I went looking for an engineer."

That had been one of Moe's dark points, when he knew, *knew*, he could turn a profit. If only he could find at least one person as a crew.

"I left the service hall discouraged. Couldn't find anyone willing to wait for their share until after I'd sold the cargo. Everyone needed the money up front." Which he understood. Truly. There were a lot of unscrupulous ship captains out there.

But Moe had never been *that guy*.

"Ended up in the bar closest to the halls, as someone had

pointed me in that direction. Atilio was there, propped up on the bar," Moe said.

At that point, Atilio had fallen onto some pretty hard times himself. It wasn't Moe's place to go into all those details. That was Atilio's story to tell.

"So we started sharing sob stories, and by the end of the evening, I'd signed him up as the chief engineer and bottle washer for *Aisha*," Moe finished up with.

Atilio had shown up at the spaceport the next morning looking ragged, his eyes bloodshot and his complexion glassy. Moe was honestly surprised to see him. He'd been expecting the other man to just ghost him.

However, Atilio had needed a job. Needed to do *something* other than to crawl into a bottle. Moe provided him with a home and structure, which Atilio had desperately needed.

And Moe got a best friend and the best mechanic he'd ever met. (He hadn't met Rosey yet, and even now, he'd still bet on Atilio in a pinch.)

"I'm glad he found you, that you found each other," Harkeen said.

"And that you found Jamaal," Moe said.

The two raised their mugs and toasted silently, each lost in their thoughts for a few moments.

Moe wasn't sure what he would have ended up doing without Atilio. He probably would have tried to make the next run on his own, and either blown himself up or been stuck somewhere out in space, unable to limp to any station.

Neither were very pleasant outcomes.

Dennis's voice brought them both out of the past and directly into the present.

"We have company," he announced.

Moe stiffened. Who'd found them? Had that damned repo ship somehow tracked them? Or was it a Kollective Defender? There were always rumors of them doing maneuvers in far space.

"I don't recognize these ships," Dennis added.

One of the walls of the breakfast nook suddenly changed into a screen.

Moe stared at the starships that now faced them. A dozen had already come in from hyperspace, with more popping in around the edges.

The one at the front was huge—as big as a Kollective Defender. The other ships ranged in size from something as big as *The Roadrunner* to as small as one of Rosey's speedships.

"I don't recognize any of those ship configurations, either," Moe said warily.

After a few moments, Dennis's voice came back online. It sounded less alive, more machine-like, than Moe had ever heard the AI use.

"You're right. Those are aliens," Dennis confirmed.

TWENTY-THREE

Wyrak "Wrong-Way" Hinga acquired his nickname when he was only a kit, having just turned eight years old. His adult fur coloration had come in that year, leaving him with a mottled look, primarily black, brown, and tan, with a white spot on his chin and another just over his right eyebrow whiskers. Golden eyes made him look wiser than he was, or so his milk-mother teased him regularly.

That year, in addition to his coat growing out, his face had broadened, so that the whiskers around his snout reached the edges of his flat cheeks instead of sticking out awkwardly past it. Plus, to keep the claws of all four of his paws trimmed, he'd graduated to an adult grinder, as his nails would now snap off instead of being soft enough to snip.

He'd also had a growth spurt that spring, and was just over one-hundred and fifty centimeters tall. (He wouldn't reach his full adult height for more than a dozen years, but eventually he'd top out at one-hundred and eighty-five centimeters.)

This meant that he was finally tall enough to join the air-bike races for kits of his age that summer, which his pack-mother reluctantly agreed to.

Of course, that first race of the season was when Wyrak started going the wrong direction.

He'd grown up in the city of Gatmil, as part of the Starclaw pack. Unlike his ancestors, modern packs were composed of a loose association of families in a geographic location, instead of all being related by blood. Other packs were formed by occupation, such as military packs, leadership packs, or even artist packs.

Mountains ranged east of the city, many of them with large untamed areas that people could hike and camp in. The race took place there, with the kits streaming away on their air-bikes one at a time, through the trees that crowded next to the trail, then up the side of the mountain.

At the top of the first hills were some designated "flying" areas, where the kits could pass each other by leaving the trail and speeding through the air. All of these gaps had reinforced nets under them. While the kits bragged about their great daring, the adults all knew they'd been safe the entire time.

The trail had clear markers, showing the kits the path they needed to use when climbing the hill.

However, when Wyrak sped down the trail, he turned right instead of left. (When asked, after all the events of the day, why he'd taken the wrong trail, he would swear that the arrow he'd seen, where the trail had split, had been pointing that direction.)

This meant that instead of quickly ascending the slope, he zig-zagged through the trees down below. He considered it a shame that no one was there to watch how cool he looked, taking the curves at crazy speeds (for his eight-year-old kit self), leaning in and nearly dumping his bike more than once.

It wasn't until he started up the slope that he began wondering if something was wrong. Surely he should be gaining on the kits who'd gone up before him. He *knew* he was faster than some of them, even though this was his first race. (Okay, so maybe he'd had to slow down some while going through the trees below. But not that much!)

No adults stood on the trail either, though. And he'd been

told that there would be adults cheering the racers on as well as ready to help all along the path.

Still, Wyrak sped on, getting winded as he climbed the fairly steep hill but gamely continuing.

Then came the first gap that he could fly over.

Warning signs proclaimed the opening, giving him plenty of time to shift gears and change the bike into flying mode. (The bike itself would have shifted once its tires left the ground, but kits didn't necessarily remember that.)

Then he was off the edge of the cliff, flying across the air, the wind blowing all his facial whiskers back, his howl of being alive and free ringing in his ears.

When he'd been thinking about the race, he'd planned out all the stunts that he'd do while he'd be in mid-air, jacking up the back wheel, turning the front wheel, doing poses and looking oh-so-cool.

However, when he looked down, he didn't see any nets.

He was certain that his pack-mother had told him there would always be something there to catch him.

No, he was really, *truly*, flying.

That made him pay all the more attention to what was beneath him: the scraggly trees, the *hard* looking yellowish rocks, the lack of any visible trail.

Something caught his eye at the far edge of the gap. Something in the crevice that didn't belong there.

Something bright and shiny and crumpled up, like an air-bike that had fallen.

When Wyrak reached the far side, he skidded to a stop.

While a part of him yowled that he needed to keep going or he was going to lose the race, he couldn't ignore what he'd seen.

He slowly put the bike down on its side, then walked back to the edge of the cliff face.

Yes, just there. He could just make out the twisted metal below him. He sniffed the cool, clear air, smelling the nearby pines and maybe a trace of machine oil.

He heard a mewling cry down below. It sent a shiver along his spine and made all the fur across his neck rise.

Without thinking about what he was doing, Wyrak reversed himself and started crawling down the edge of the cliff, not caring how much dirt he ground under his claws or how it was getting rubbed into the fur on his arms.

Partway down the hill he came to the crash site.

An older female lay there, crying quietly. Blood matted her brown-and-white facial fur. She held her right arm up across her chest, the paw dangling at an odd, broken angle.

She gave a howl of joy when he came into view. "I saw you! Flying above me! I wondered if you were a star-angel, come to rescue me!"

Wyrak shrugged awkwardly. He was no superhero coming in to save the day. He was just a kit.

Still, he had faithfully attended all the Kit Scout meetings that his pack-mother sent him to the past few years, learning how to bandage a broken limb or treat a fire wound. (He'd learned as an adult to let the professionals handle the latter. Particularly the deep skin burns. Sparks could burn off all of someone's fur. Luckily, fur was meant to be sacrificed, and though someone might be naked and fur-less for a while, it took a very serious fire to damage the tough skin underneath.)

So he bound up the female's arm (Kausis, as she insisted he call her though she was easily twenty years his senior), immobilizing it so that they could start the long climb back to the top of the cliff.

It wasn't easy. Even as an adult, Wyrak could look back and appreciate that the climb would have been strenuous even for anyone, even without a second person who he'd had to help every step of the way. Not that it was steps, but a series of toe- and claw-holds that he'd sometimes had to scratch out of the dirt.

It took them most of the rest of the day to get to the top, mainly because of the number of stops they'd had to make along the way. Then he set Kausis up on his bike, balancing her there while he pushed it along the trail, hoping that the path they were on looped around to the main trail at some point.

Luckily, the rest of the kits had finished the race by then and the adults had organized a search party for him.

Of course, the other kits tended to by his pack-mother teased him for missing the race, for coming in last, for going the wrong direction.

However, Kausis insisted that he get a reward for going the wrong direction and finding her, buying him a custom-made air-bike. She proclaimed that he had a third paw—an invisible paw of fate—that had pressed down on him at the exact right moment.

She might have been a crazy female who'd lain there for several hours, in pain and unable to rescue herself.

Or she may have been onto something, particularly as others claimed to have seen that third paw of his in action, more than once.

Despite the nickname "Wrong-Way," or maybe because of it, Wyrak applied to be a navigator when the war started. He had just begun college but honestly, didn't have a trail that he felt compelled to follow. Most of his class- and clan-mates were much more driven than he was.

Whereas Wyrak drifted along, fate giving him a path as much as anything else.

The problem was that Wyrak was *terrible* at figuring out which direction he was going in. He took to wearing a small leather bracelet around his left wrist so that he'd remember which way that was. (He may have initially tried tying one around his left ankle for the same reason, though that hadn't been as successful.)

Of course, his new packmates, that is, the collection of people that he was housed with, who'd also joined the military and were taking classes, teased him mercilessly about it once they saw it. Particularly those who'd shared his navigation classes.

Wyrak stubbornly persisted. Fortunately, he was better at doing the necessary math calculations than many of the others. He did have issues showing his work, as frequently the number just came to him and he'd have to start with the answer and work his way backwards in order to prove that he'd intuited the correct solution.

It was only during military training, with the correct physical exercises, that Wyrak finally figured out what part of his "navigation" problem was.

Ninety-nine percent of his people, the Lithic, were left-pawed.

He was right-pawed. He'd certainly learned to do everything with his left paw, as no one had ever bothered trying to teach him otherwise.

But honestly, once he started using his right paw more, things became easier for him.

He graduated at the bottom of his class, something about getting lost and not being able to find the hall where the first final was being held. It took him three tries to pass the exam that allowed him to work as a navigator on a military spaceship. Then, it took another year of flying local routes in his own system before he passed the next exam and acquired the rank of pack navigator, third-class. That was the lowest class allowed to fly in a starship.

Wyrak was assigned to the Night Pack squadron, which was one of the three squadrons that made up the Star Pack fleet. The ships that made up a fleet were a single Predator, three heavily-armed Battle Cruisers (one for each squadron), a dozen (or more) Lancers and Maulers, at least three times that many Darts for close combat, and Suppliers drifting in and out to keep the squadron well-stocked, as well as to carry away the wounded.

Wyrak's initial fear that he'd be assigned a Supplier and never see battle had been unfounded. Instead, he started off on the Lancer *Six-Claw* in the Night Pack squadron. The energy weapons associated with this type of ship tended to be longer-range than a Mauler's, so while he was able to be in a battle, he was still a little off to the side, not in the thick of it.

Until, of course, he flicked the wrong switch. Or did the wrong calculation. Or whatever it was that he'd accidentally done, so that when *Six-Claw* did its next hyperspace hop, instead of staying on the edges of a battle, the ship landed right in the middle of everything.

Crap.

"Keep firing! Keep firing!" his lancer captain had commanded.

Though the person responsible for the guns (who sat right next to Wyrak on the bridge) sent a seething glare at him, she did, indeed, keep firing.

Which gave Wyrak a crazy thought about a maneuver that had never been tried before.

Instead of setting up the next hyperspace jump, he set *Six-Claw* to spin on its center axis, slicing one of the large Mind ships in half (and luckily, missing the Darts who'd closed on the enemy ships).

He had the Lancer do two full rotations as he plotted out the next hyperspace jump and got them out of there.

Six-Claw had taken some damage while they'd been in the midst of things, something that his captain was not very pleased about.

One of the primary enemy ships, though, had been destroyed, Wyrak's maneuver turning the tide of the battle.

He'd received a medal and commendations from high command, though he was still a third class navigator. After a couple more accidents of this nature, some of the crew started considering him their "luck" and tried to refuse to go into battle unless he was on the bridge. (The captain didn't think highly of such shenanigans. Not even when Wrong-Way sent them in the opposite direction one flight, and instead of joining the battle they'd been assigned to, ended up saving an entire planet from a surprise attack.)

News of Wyrak's misadventures reached the ears of the fleet commander, Jiac Beowen. She would be hard-pressed, later, to explain why she'd agreed to the promotion of Wyrak "Wrong-Way" Hinga, allowing him to work as a navigator on the Predator *Nightfall*.

In her defense, the rest of the crew did consider him *lucky*, three-pawed, with that invisible paw of fate weighing down on his choices regularly.

And quite frankly, the Star Pack fleet could use some luck. As could the entire Lithic people, though that sort of bad news regarding the war generally wasn't shared beyond the upper echelon of officers.

Officially, Wyrak was still part of the Night Pack squadron. He reported up that chain of command, through Omyk Mangress, who was the leader of the squadron.

But for now, Wyrak lived on *Nightfall*, and worked from her bridge.

So far, he'd only once messed up, sending the Predator on what turned out to be a wild-mouse chase across system, following a ghost signal on his screen that was supposedly an enemy ship. (Later, her engineers had assured her that their equipment was so well tuned nothing like a ghost-signal could be generated, that Wrong-Way had made the entire thing up.) Instead of finding this enemy, they'd run across a Supplier who'd suffered a catastrophic failure in their core engines and was just barely creeping along.

During their most recent battle, more than one of the Darts had been badly damaged. As was SOP, they'd sent out communications to their respective squadron leaders that they were doing a short hyperspace hop and would be waiting at one of the nearby rendezvous points.

Nightfall and the rest of the fleet had emerged at a location that, as far as Jiac could tell, wasn't anywhere near any of the agreed upon spots.

However.

The two ships in front of them were *not* of Lithic manufacture.

Nor were they enemy ships.

Jiac felt her head fall into her waiting palm, covering her entire face.

"Wrong-Way, where have you brought us to now?"

TWENTY-FOUR

Not for the first time, Jun wished she could clone herself.

First of all, there were all the fantastic papers from Lawaka, all the new information she'd learned about the Atoylee, about the bomb they'd been building, the enemy they'd been fighting.

The *alien* enemy.

Then *Aisha* had arrived at the new system and had found yet *another* alien ship. Rosey swore that despite its size, it was actually a starship, able to travel through hyperspace.

They'd found another data core. This one was less damaged, and Sano had managed to pull a *lot* more information from it.

The ship itself was able to give them clues as to which words meant what, with a full control panel. Many of the controls had words printed on them. Rosey and Atilio had given her their best estimate on what the words meant, deciphering what the various gauges measured.

There was so much work to do on the new aliens. And their language! And the Atoylee!

Jun had come to rely on Moe to tell her when to eat, as well as when to go to bed. Sano would reinforce his suggestions if she ignored them. But she was much less pleasant about it.

Plus, having meals with everyone meant that she could spend time with the others, bouncing ideas off them, like a real team.

Honestly, despite her frustration of too many questions, too much work, and not enough hours in the day that they'd set up, this was one of the most fulfilling experiences of her life.

Then actual, *living aliens* had shown up.

A very large, very well-armed group of them.

Sano and Dennis set to figure out how to communicate with the various ships, focusing their attention on the big Defender-like vessel.

Rosey, Atilio, and Jamaal were all having a quiet conversation to one side, counting the number of guns and not liking their odds.

She didn't care much for their odds of shooting their way out, either.

However, she *was* a princess. That meant that she'd been trained to be an ambassador. She knew both planetary as well as intergalactic law better than all the rest of them put together.

And she could, in a pinch, claim to be a representative of one of the three primary Human governments. The Emperor would back her up. She was certain of it.

They were all gathered together in one of Rosey's workshops. Dennis huffily came on the speaker.

"I've figured out the visuals," he said. "Their systems are stupid, though."

"So no AIs?" Jun inquired. Did they not have the technology?

"It's a military ship. They wouldn't rely on an AI system," Jamaal said.

"Much easier to carry more grunts and train them to run everything, rather than have an AI and take a chance on it getting damaged during a fight," Atilio added.

So they might have AI capability, just not be using it on these ships.

"But you managed to connect our visual systems?" Jun said.

"I have," Dennis said, now sounding smug. "And communication systems as well. So what do you want as a backdrop? Something majestic, like the Emperor's throne room?"

"No, no, not like that," Jun said. "That won't give the right impression. We need to appear as friendly, not as threatening. We want informal negotiations for now, not formal. Not yet."

"Fine," Dennis said. "I suppose you want a backdrop of *beige*."

Jun took a quick look at the assembled group. "How about a soft rosy color?" she asked.

"I can do that," Dennis said, sounding mollified.

"No sparkling effects or glitter," Rosey warned.

"Just a touch of shimmer in the background, to make it interesting," Dennis assured them.

"Let's not keep our potential partners waiting, shall we?" Jun said, stepping in before Rosey and Dennis could argue any more.

The image on the screen in front of them resolved slowly.

It was being broadcast from the helm of the warship. One main person sat in a large chair in the center of the room, while other crew members worked at stations surrounding the central figure.

The people though...wow.

They were *lion-like* people. Cats had flatter faces, whereas lions had more of a protruding snout. No mane, though. Covered in fur of all different colors. Their eyes were proportionately larger in their faces than a Human's. Whiskers hung from their snouts as well as stuck out from their eyebrows. Ear jutted up from the tops of their head, and appeared to be able to rotate.

The uniforms they wore had different colors. Did that indicate rank? Or field of responsibility? Beyond the color they were roughly the same: loose shirts going up to the neck with long, closely-fit sleeves that ended mid-arm, showing a furry forearm and wrist, the backs of the hands covered in the same fur while the palms were clear. Though Jun would bet that they were tall, they were also long-waisted, with shorter legs, the pants going all the way down to their boots. Bipedal, with only two arms.

She couldn't help but check. They didn't appear to have tails, though.

Jun stepped forward, addressing the person sitting on the chair. That person had primarily white fur with orange spots across their face and arms. Green eyes with a vertical pupil considered her warily.

"Human," Jun said, indicating herself and all the people standing behind her. "Humans," she said, repeating the gestures.

The other person nodded. "Lithic," they said, using similar gestures, including themself and the others around them.

Jun patted her chest and said, "Jun." She repeated the motion and the word a couple of times. Then she gave her full title. "Princess Jun Ogawa, from the court of Emperor Ogawa." She knew that the other person wouldn't understand, but she wanted more words from the other person. Sano was still trying to negotiate a language exchange with their computers, but couldn't get through.

The other person replied with, "Jiac." They paused, then added more, words that Jun couldn't identify.

Yet.

"Atilio. Jamaal. Do one of you have a stunner, blaster, or gun that you can break down, take apart?" Jun said quietly without looking away from Jiac. "I need to show them that we come in peace."

Just taking a weapon and tossing it onto the ground wouldn't do it. That might be the equivalent for the Lithic of throwing down the gauntlet and declaring war.

Atilio stepped up, beside Jun. He held up a gun-shaped stunner.

Jiac nodded, appearing to understand what it was he was holding.

Jun couldn't read the alien's body language, but the other person appeared to be holding themselves more stiffly than they had been.

Atilio broke the stunner apart, quickly removing the charge

cartridge, sliding off the barrel, removing the trigger. He handed the pieces to Jun and stepped back.

Jun lifted the pieces up and looked Jiac directly in their eyes. "We come in peace," she said.

The words meant nothing.

Hopefully the gesture would be understood.

Jiac tilted their head to one side.

Jun couldn't help but smile. The gesture may or may not have been one of curiosity, but it certainly looked that way to her Human eyes.

Jiac looked around at the people on their helm. Their eyes lighted on one of the people seated in front of them. They raised one arm and pointed at this person, saying something that to Jun's ears, sounded accusatory.

The other person's eyes widened and they put both hands to their chest, a clear "Who, me?" reaction if Jun had ever seen one.

Jiac gave a sharp nod.

Oh thank all the ancestors. It appeared that the Lithic nodded when they meant yes. No idea if they shook their head for, "No," but Jun couldn't wait to find out.

The other person stood up. Jun didn't know what the scale was on their ship, but this person appeared to be tall. They walked up closer to the display and carefully studied Jun and her companions. This person's fur was mottled—black, brown, and tan—with white patches on their chin and just above their right eye whiskers.

It surprised Jun that they then paused for a moment. Closed their golden eyes and bowed their head.

Were they praying? Paying respects to some distant relative?

When the person looked up again, they seemed determined.

They pointed to Jun, Jamaal, Moe, and Rosey. Then they waved their hand, with the fingers pointed down.

When Jun didn't nod, the person pointed to those same people again, walked away, then made the same motion again, with the fingers pointed down, only more firmly.

Ah. This person wanted them to come over to their ship.

"Thoughts?" Jun said quietly.

"Stretchsuits with extra oxygen," Jamaal said immediately. "We don't know if their air is breathable. Or what it'll smell like."

"Is this a good idea?" Atilio said. "They could decide to kill you without warning."

"I understand that this is likely a military venture," Jun counted with. "That means that they probably have laws and structures when it comes to killing, and won't do it indiscriminately."

Or so she hoped.

Of course, her people would be armed. And even without some sort of weapon, she was aware that Jamaal was deadly all on his own.

Hopefully, it would never come down to that.

TWENTY-FIVE

Itsuki sat in his lair, going through his reports.

It wasn't that he had an evil palace of doom that he retreated to. No, it was a perfectly functional office with a comfortable work chair, a rather sophisticated computer desk, and an altar to the Fire God that he supposedly represented in the corner.

However, Itsuki was the spy master for the Emperor. He likened himself and his situation to that of a spider, with him sitting in the center of his web, always diligently aware of the slightest trembling along any of the long lines.

Most of the time, Itsuki preferred to receive all the information from his various minions aurally. Though the lair itself was sound-proof, Itsuki had a bonephone implanted on his collarbone, and he listened to all the reports on that.

That habit allowed him to walk around the office, slowly, meditatively pacing. He'd always found that being in motion, instead of trying to sit still, enabled him to stay more focused and alert. Plus, his ears caught things that his eyes didn't. He might make assumptions about the intent of the person reporting if he relied on reading.

Listening, nuances were clearer. As were the gaps.

At first, he'd assumed that Jamaal had escaped from the

(admittedly clumsy) attempt to detain him through chance alone. Rosey had been under attack, and must have called him.

It wasn't until later Itsuki realized that Jamaal and his lover Harkeen were on the move long before Rosey had been contacted by the punks who'd tried to take her out.

Jamaal hadn't been trying to hide as he'd walked across the space station *Lorenzo*. No, he stuck to very populated areas. He didn't seem to care about the number of cameras that might have captured his location.

And both Jamaal as well as Harkeen carried bags. Small ones, for a short overnight stay somewhere.

Had someone warned Jamaal of the warrant being issued for his arrest?

Itsuki mulled that over as he continued applying pressure to that idiot Constantine. The warlord had been ridiculously easy to manipulate. All it had taken was a few credits, discreetly placed in his accounts. Then, Constantine did all the dirty work of blackmailing the bank into immediately calling in the loan note for *Aisha*.

The repo ship had come back empty-handed, though. The bank had a standard operating procedure for dealing with that. The penalties for disabling the bank clock on a ship were astronomical, at least for a little trader like Moe.

He'd be out of the picture soon enough. Though Moe, or more likely his sidekick, Atilio, had removed all the trackers that Itsuki had so carefully placed on the starship, they would have to resupply the ship at some point.

And no station was going to disobey a priority alert from the Empire. Not in any of the systems.

All Itsuki had to know was the location of the ship. "Pirates" would take care of the rest.

And if Jun wasn't killed during that battle, she'd be sure to come back to Ishiman to mourn. And Itsuki would get another chance at her.

While Rosey would make a good target to get at Jamaal, she

appeared to already have her own haters. Whoever it was, though, was good at hiding their tracks. He could see the echoes of their fingerprints, feel them in the trembling of his web.

How deeply did he dig into his rival, as it were? Did he seek them out in order to make common cause? He suspected their pockets were as deep as his, but they were also operating from a distance, through third parties.

Nothing to be done at the moment.

Except to clean his own house.

Someone had to have warned Jamaal.

And when he found out who, well, he would have his revenge on them as well.

TWENTY-SIX

Jamaal had had hopes. Dreams even, of making live contact, with actual living aliens.

The reality was both better and worse than he could have ever imagined.

They took a flitter from *The Roadrunner* over to the large (alien!) vessel. The airlocks weren't compatible, so they had a quick walk in space from their ship to the other.

Lights flashed all around them after they entered the airlock, before the inner door was open. A sonic cleaner, perhaps? Decontamination of some sort?

While Jamaal knew that the airlock itself was alien, it appeared that physics were physics, and there wasn't really anything new or different from an alien point of view.

It wasn't until the far door cycled, and Jamaal was in the presence of an actual, *living alien*, that his heart rate skyrocketed and his palms began to sweat, even in the stretchsuit that he wore.

The Lithic were tall. Their guide was the same height as Jamaal, at least six feet, and that person appeared to be about average, with some of the nearby people bigger and only one smaller.

Sano announced through their comms that the air was breathable.

Jamaal immediately reached up and retracted his helmet. The eyes of the alien watching him grew very large. At least the goons standing behind the front person didn't react in the slightest, beyond a slight tensing.

After a big sniff, Jamaal nodded to the others, so they retracted their helmets as well.

The air was well filtered, but there was still a musty scent. Did that come from the aliens themselves, possibly because of all that fur? Jamaal didn't know and knew that he couldn't possibly ask.

The hallway they stood in struck Jamaal as generic military. The walls, ceiling, and floor were all made from metal painted a light gray. Lights shone down from recessed cans in the ceiling.

Dennis would have proclaimed it *beige*.

However, it was well maintained. No scuff marks marring the paint. The floor was clean. No cobwebs up in the corners.

"Hello," Jun said. She gave a smile to the main alien, the one with the golden eyes, without showing her teeth. She'd been very clear in her instructions that they shouldn't appear threatening at all, not until they were threatened themselves.

The alien replied with something short, that probably meant the same thing.

"I am Jun," she said, pressing her hand to her chest. "Jun Ogawa." Then she introduced the rest of them.

The alien repeated their names, then said their own.

Wyrak. Wyrak Hinga, if Jamaal was hearing this person correctly.

One of the guards suggested another name for Wyrak, something that prefaced their name.

Wyrak rolled their eyes and waved their hand, dismissing the suggestion.

Their guide appeared lost for a moment, then shrugged, turned and made that same motion that meant, "Follow me."

Wyrak led them to what appeared to be a conference room. The chairs and table were all recognizable. Wyrak stepped to the far side of the table and sat down on the middle of the long side.

Jun sat directly across from Wyrak, while Jamaal and the others spread themselves out. He didn't like sitting with his back to the only door to the room, but he didn't have much choice. He still sat as far away from the door as he could, so he would have a few more moments to react in case of an attack.

The chairs had to be pulled out from under the table. They had an automated latching system, so they wouldn't float away if the ship lost gravity. So while they had artificial gravity—it appeared to be slightly heavier than the standard that Humans used—it also was something mechanical that could break.

Good to know.

The walls were the same gray as the hallway, though the floor now had some sort of carpet, a sandy brown color. No designs covered the walls, no artwork or decorations.

Dennis would definitely be complaining non-stop at this point.

Jamaal had agreed with Jun that Sano shouldn't announce her presence, that she should just use the comms to speak to them. Jun had been equipped with an earpiece, so she could hear the AI.

He'd bet that Sano was prompting Jun, having her repeat what Wyrak had said when their guide had first seen them, saying the equivalent of, "Hello."

They didn't have the vocabulary to talk. Not really. Sano and Dennis were piecing things together as quickly as they could. Some sort of primer from the Lithic would really help.

Was Wyrak also wearing a comm device? So that they could be prompted as well? Difficult to tell, given ears on top of their head that had fur sticking out of them. Maybe they had an embedded bonephone like Rosey did.

Then, Jun pulled out the first data core, the one that was more damaged and had less information.

Wyrak sat up stiffly, staring hard at the glowing crystal.

Jun just started talking. "We found this in a *thulin*," she said.

"*Thuylin*," Wyrak automatically corrected.

Jamaal couldn't help but beam at Jun's joy.

They had figured out a word. And the word had been correct.

Jamaal felt as though he might actually burst.

Harkeen was going to tease him so hard when he retold this story.

However, he was still going to talk about it, possibly forever at this point.

Jun pushed the data core across the table to Wyrak. After a lot of pantomime, she managed to get across that they'd like a transcript of what was on it.

Wyrak seemed hesitant.

Jamaal understood. This *thuylin* had been a military ship. There might be data on it that the military considered sensitive.

In addition to the leather bracelet that Wyrak wore around their left wrist, they also had something that looked like a multifunction watch. They spoke into the device and appeared to receive an okay from whoever was on the other end, because they nodded and handed the data core to one of the guards standing behind him, who accepted it with a shrug, then left the room.

During the charades a whiteboard had been acquired. Rosey now took it upon herself to draw out an accurate representation of the control panel from the ship they'd found. Dennis was probably talking with her, prompting her to write out the words on the gauges.

Wyrak's eyes grew wide again and they nodded sharply. They talked to the comm on their wrist again, then turned to the rest of them, ignoringRosey.

Maybe Wyrak had figured out that Rosey was their engineer, and there wasn't much that they could help her with.

They got more whiteboards, and Moe tried drawing the helm of a ship, with him in the chair, to let Wyrak know what it was he did. While they were in the middle of that, another person joined them.

This person introduced themselves as Nysh Pushi. They were shorter than Wyrak, but the way they moved reminded Jamaal of a predator, wiry muscles and sleek grace. Their fur was primarily gray with black stripes. They also had the brightest blue eyes that Jamaal had ever seen.

Were they natural? Or did the Lithic have genetic engineering?

Jamaal didn't know if there were sexual characteristics that defined male and female among the Lithic, or if they even had just two sexes. However, he'd be willing to bet that Nysh was female, based on the nipples pushing up their shirt.

All six of them.

After the introduction, Nysh ignored the rest of them, sitting down across from Rosey and staring at the control panel. They started to talk to each other, quickly building some sort of engineer's pidgin.

As Jamaal was trying to explain the concept of buying and selling goods just through pictures without a shared vocabulary, the first guard came back in with what looked like papers in their hand that they handed to Jun.

She beamed at everyone and went through them slowly, page by page, Sano probably scanning them immediately.

Then Jun tried to read some of what was on the page out loud.

Wyrak corrected her again and again. They shook their head at one point.

Jamaal would bet Wyrak was complaining about Jun's accent.

It was thrilling to be here on an alien ship. It was mundane to be trying to figure out each other's language.

He couldn't help but be smugly satisfied that it was he and his team who'd gotten here first.

He had the bragging rights of the century, now.

He couldn't wait to rub it in Duri Chung's face. As well as all the disbelievers out there.

TWENTY-SEVEN

Duri could not believe what she was seeing on the report handed to her by the military research team.

There was a *second* site that the Atoylee had occupied? On the closer of the two moons orbiting Niani?

And no one had mounted an expedition there?

Of course, this information had only just been made public. It would be difficult to get together a research team in such a short amount of time.

Duri had no such difficulty, though.

A quick call into General Carrick got her the funds (because she wasn't about to spend *her* department's money on this). Choosing the archaeologists turned out to be more difficult, not because she had no one to pick from but because she had too many qualified candidates.

Eventually she built up a team where at least half the people had strong ties to the Kollective government in one way or another, while the other half were pure academics whose only loyalty would be to the truth.

In less than a week, Duri had the ultimate decision facing her.

Did she go with them? Or just send them out?

What if they didn't find anything? Wouldn't that be a colossal waste of her time?

The numbers didn't add up. She told herself that she could always go on a second ship, after the first.

Her gut told her otherwise.

Something was there.

Something big.

So in the end, after two frantic weeks of work, Duri found herself standing in a small room on the starship *Examiner* with not much to do.

It would take the ship a few days to reach Niani. Once there, they'd go into orbit around Lawaka, doing penetrative scans of the moon.

Maybe they'd find something.

Or maybe Duri would end up with egg on her face.

The die was cast as she felt the ship slip into hyperspace.

For better or worse, she was committed.

Duri couldn't help her feelings of vindication when the initial scans came back positive. They still merely orbited the moon, but they'd found it.

There *was* a base there, on Lawaka, buried deep beneath the surface.

Duri let the experts and a military team go first, though they'd set up a live feed, so that she and the others on the ship could see what they discovered.

The door leading to the base stood partially open. This told Duri that someone else had been there, before them. The experts at the table with her agreed.

They would have seen such an opening before now. One of the geeks even brought up an earlier image, proving that the door had been shut earlier, no hole appearing in that rock.

Then came the first images of the hallway.

It wasn't natural. Everyone could agree on that.

The elevator room was a marvel. Duri wasn't the only one who gasped. One of the people beside her immediately started enhancing and improving the feed as it was broadcast, doing a side-by-side comparison, showing the vivid colors as they'd once been.

Amazing.

Though Duri had always been focused on contact with living aliens, seeing an alien habitat that hadn't been destroyed still made her heart sing.

They found the door and started going down the stairs. Duri approved of how solidly the structure had been manufactured. Nothing short of a direct hit would take out these stairs.

Eventually, the connection was lost, as the team had gotten too deep underground and out of range. Possibly there was some sort of shielding that had been built into the walls as well.

The military wanted to stop at that point.

Duri overrode the commander, forcing them onward.

She was glad she did, when they reported back just a short while later, showing the recordings of the base below.

Duri gave them their orders to take samples of absolutely everything, then report back to the ship.

It was her turn to go explore.

The climb down the stairs hadn't been too awful. Then again, Duri had tried to stay in shape, despite having a desk job. Her legs still felt wobbly when she reached the bottom.

She blamed her lack of breath on her descent, not wanting to admit just how *amazing* this base was.

The empty file cabinets they found, though, enraged her.

At one point, they had held something. Something important.

Other people had been here and stripped this site clean.

Duri could see their footprints in the dust that had once been carpet. More than one artifact had been disturbed, samples already collected.

Everything was decaying and breaking down.

Her engineers guessed that the machinery that had protected the base, given it some sort of atmosphere, had probably broken down only recently, which was why everything was in such good shape.

Still. The laws governing an alien find were clear.

Whoever had been here first were no better than grave robbers. They should have notified the intergalactic community as soon as they'd found this base. The best and the brightest minds should have had a crack at this material before it had decayed further.

And Duri had a good idea of exactly who had done this.

Princess Jun. Rosey. Jamaal. The others.

The only thing that ameliorated her anger was her glee at being able to present her findings. Not even being a princess would save Jun. And the others had no such prestige to draw on, to protect them.

She was going to have to prove that they'd been here first. Fortunately, she'd had clear recordings made of the footprints left by others, before her team had arrived. (One of the military people had insisted on doing that first. Duri was going to have to figure out how to reward him later.)

Just the footprints weren't much, but put those with together with the repo ship finding *Aisha* here, and she might have enough circumstantial evidence to at least question that group under oath.

All she had to do at that point was to find some of the alien artifacts. She would have to set up searches with all the sites she knew of, that she regularly had contact with, that sold alien artifacts on the black market.

Most of the artifacts were fake.

However, this base would give rise to some real ones, soon enough.

Duri had her engineers take apart the machine in the closet that had probably been generating the atmosphere for the local area. Most of the pieces crumbled to dust in their hands.

The power source, though, was still encased in a box composed of a diamond-like material. It emitted a radioactive signal through the portholes at the base, though very weak, just a trickle.

Duri would bet that the object itself was still an incredibly powerful battery. The weakness of the signal was just due to shielding, not due to the power source losing its juice.

Of course, Humans already had such technology. Much better than this, actually. However, it proved that the Atoylee were more advanced than anyone had thought before now.

Unless they'd had alien help.

That was one of the things that her people had uncovered, or at least had speculated about. That the Atoylee had, in fact, had some contact with a different alien species.

Had they helped the Atoylee set up this base?

Possibly.

Or possibly the other theory was true—that the Atoylee were in fact under attack from an alien species, and were developing bombs up here.

Duri didn't like the implications of that.

An alien super weapon in the hands of one of the other Human governments, outside of the control of the Kollective, had long been a source of nightmares.

Still, Duri tried to enjoy her time there at an alien base, aware that she would be one of the last to pass through as it crumbled around her. Her own scientists were attempting to set up some environmental controls to save at least one of the rooms: a common area that had magnificent geometric patterns on the walls, a few couches and chairs rapidly decaying.

She didn't know if they'd be successful. She almost hoped

they wouldn't be, so that she'd have yet another crime to lay at the feet of that group of criminals.

The princess. Rosey. Jamaal. Even that loafer of a starship captain, Moe.

Duri left the base and walked back up flight after flight of stairs, making plans and plotting her revenge.

TWENTY-EIGHT

Ajax awkwardly adjusted the T-shirt with the goofy cartoon character on it and pushed his greasy hair out of his eyes.

He had to sell this part to the station manager on *Lorenzo.*

They sat in the manager's office. It was plush in a sort of generic way, with thick carpet, ugly modern art that some designer had picked out, and sleek furniture that was all chrome and leather and uncomfortable.

Erin Gratski—the manager—had seen better days. She was ancient (probably over sixty!) with spiky gray hair tinted green on the ends, matching green eyeshadow (ugh) and bright red lipstick.

Fortunately, she wasn't the brightest star in the cluster.

It helped that at one point, he had been such a fan of Rosey De Vries. He could talk about the important races she'd won, the speedships she'd developed.

He was just a fan. When he heard the news, he couldn't believe it. Not Rosey! So he was here to help her out.

Honest.

The station needed to do something with her space. She'd broken the law as far as they were concerned. There were rumors that she'd endangered people with her workshop, at least according to the latest reports from the Racing Oversight committee.

There had also been accusations made about her cheating, not following all the rules when it came to building her speedships.

Though Rosey did have a good reputation, there were plenty of sore losers out there who evidently could be bought.

Whoever was doing the social assassination on Rosey had deep pockets, and plenty of ire.

Possibly Duri Chung was behind all of it. Ajax wouldn't put it past the bitch. She might have given off "cute Asian girl" vibes, but he'd looked too closely in her eyes.

Colder than vacuum. Meaner than a pirate cheated out of his payday.

And sneakier than a crooked bookkeeper who had three sets of books: one for the government, one for the company, and one for himself that showed how much he was actually skimming from the accounts.

Now, all Ajax had to do was to get this Erin to sign over Rosey's workshop to him, put it in some sort of protectorate.

"I have had other offers for the space," Erin let Ajax know. "Developers who want to create more housing for the station."

"I know that space is limited on *Lorenzo*," Ajax said, still projecting confidence. "But I'm sure that once Rosey comes back, she'll be able to clear all this up!"

That may have been a little too enthusiastic, as Erin's eyebrows climbed.

"And you don't know where she is," Erin asked again, leaning back in her own chair.

Maybe that was how to make the torture piece he was sitting on more comfortable.

He tried leaning back himself, but that just brought more pain to his back.

Nope. Barely touching the chair was the way to go. Let it support his butt and nothing else.

"I don't know where she is," Ajax said. He had some thoughts on the matter.

She'd probably deciphered enough of those alien artifacts to find alien space. Ajax knew better than to underestimate her.

He'd done that once. The results hadn't been disastrous, but only because Ajax had been able to work a deal with Constantine.

Though his parents were sending him increasingly distraught messages, insisting that he come home and take some responsibility.

He figured he'd have to at least make a token payment to them at some point.

After he finished this little job for Constantine, doing so well he'd be promoted in the ranks of Constantine's employees. Possibly brought in as second in command.

Yeap. That was what Ajax deserved for all this play-acting he was doing.

Ajax could tell that Erin wasn't necessarily buying his innocent routine.

"I know that she's had some sort of ugly run in with some pirates, out in Allied Worlds' space," Ajax continued conspiratorially. "Even ran a race out there."

He assumed that everyone would know about his race with Rosey at this point. Didn't matter that he'd lost. He'd still been in competition with her, which only the best of the best could claim at this point.

"That was long before this matter," Erin said dismissively.

"She might still be having some sort of dealings with them," Ajax said. "But I really don't know for certain."

Erin looked at him for another long moment before glancing back at the contract on her desk.

"All right. So you want to take over Rosey's contract with the station, at least for now," Erin said. "Then, after Rosey gets back, you might sell it back to her? If she's been cleared of all wrongdoing?"

"Exactly!" Ajax said, beaming. "I don't want her workshop destroyed."

No, not until after she returned. Then she could watch him take everything apart. Watch every piece as it sold for fractions of a credit, nowhere near what it was actually worth.

Watch helplessly as Ajax tore her world apart.

Because that was what Constantine wanted. For Rosey to suffer.

Ajax was certain that the warlord had the others in his sights as well.

He couldn't wait to be part of their destruction.

It took most of the rest of the morning, with Ajax continuing to play the part of just helping out. Eventually, though, after a couple of small changes to the contract—more oversight for the station manager, basically—they worked out the details to Ajax's satisfaction.

He happily received the lockout codes for Rosey's workshop.

Boy, was she in for a surprise when she finally returned.

He couldn't wait.

TWENTY-NINE

Rosey entered the conference room on the alien ship *Nightfall*, their usual guard, Cali, striding behind her. Wyrak was already there, sipping the Lithic's equivalent of coffee. (Though Dennis had examined it and rated it harmless, that hadn't accounted for the god-awful taste. Rosey's stomach still churned at the thought of it.)

She smiled at him, and his whiskers rose, their equivalent of a smile.

It had been three long, hard days of work. Rosey hadn't gotten much sleep. Then again, neither had anyone else.

After greeting him in his language, and getting a fairly understandable greeting in the Human common tongue, she brought out her prize and placed it on the conference table.

It wasn't the prettiest piece of equipment that she'd ever hacked together. She still needed more base chemicals for her 3D printer, so the housing was an ugly matte black.

However, when Rosey spoke, asking Wyrak again how he was, the translator repeated the words in the Lithic language. The voice was similar to Dennis's, though not as alive.

Wyrak's eye whiskers rose toward the top of his head. He said something in his own language, which the translator repeated in common. "What is this?"

Rosey smiled and nodded. It was something of a pain to have to wait for the translator to finish. And it lost its place if Rosey tried reading a page from a spec without a break. No, a couple of paragraphs was all the poor thing could handle at this point.

However, the programming was solid, or at least Jun as well as Sano had assured her.

"It's a translator," Rosey said.

She brought out a second one, identical to the first.

Wyrak contacted Kalesen on his wristcomm, an engineer that Rosey had worked with before, asking him to come down and talk with them.

Rosey nodded, happy that her understanding of the conversation had been in line with the translation that she heard from the machine once Wyrak finished.

When Kalesen came in, Rosey went with him to the end of the table with the second translator as well as the specs on the device.

The Lithic did have AI, but as Jamaal and Atilio had speculated, it wasn't allowed on a military ship in any capacity. There seemed to be some bad history there that Rosey hadn't bothered digging into.

Sano was the only reason they'd been able to come up with a translator so quickly. Rosey and the others hadn't confessed to the presence of an AI, though Wyrak and presumably his command must have assumed that there was one.

Particularly after they understood that Jun worked as a xeno-linguist. In addition to being a princess, which had been an entire afternoon of charades.

Kalesen easily followed along with the wiring of the translator. That was one place where the Lithic were far in advance of the Humans—they'd had a breakthrough in terms of fiber optics that the Humans never had. This meant their wiring was a lot more fine, as well as able to handle a bigger load.

All the externals of the translator could be easily copied.

It was the internals, the software, that was the true heart of the thing.

Rosey had learned to not give away much. Sure, the first taste was always free. But after that, well, there was always a cost.

"Yes, you can have the translator," Rosey told Kalesen. "But it won't do you much good unless you can figure out the computer software."

Kalesen listened to the translation and nodded. "We need to develop a common computer language," he said. "Something that will take advantage of all of our tech."

"Exactly," Rosey said.

That had been the one thing that she'd most enjoyed about dealing with the Lithic. They appeared to be fairly reasonable. Sure, there were going to be assholes in every culture. But Jiac ran a tight fleet, and she seemed to understand that friendly alien contact was likely to get them further than unfriendly.

The plan for today, now that they had a translator, was to push that.

Rosey was still a little uncertain of the wisdom of that. However, Jun had shown herself to be an excellent ambassador so far.

When Jun had tried to ask why the Lithic were flying around in a military fleet, Wyrak had pretended to not understand their question. That was the good as well as bad thing about charades.

However, the signs were all there. The Lithic were probably at war with someone.

Who, though?

Jun had a plan to find out.

As Rosey and Kalesen hammered out some of the initial exchanges of software between the two races, Jun and Jamaal showed up.

Jamaal was the happiest that Rosey had ever seen him. He'd even put on a fighting demonstration in one of the gyms on the ship a few days before.

The Lithic were fierce warriors, who had range on Jamaal. However, even Rosey could see that their forms were all top heavy. They didn't do many kicks. During the demonstration, Jamaal was able to hold them off with his legs. He was already in collaboration with one of the military people about coming up with a new fighting form that took their hand-to-hand style and mixed it with some of the Human forms.

Though Moe wasn't there that day (by design), he had started meeting with the fleet steward, seeing what supplies the Lithic normally carried, what they wanted and needed, setting the basis for a trade network between the two peoples.

Not that the Humans knew where exactly the Lithic home systems were.

Rosey would bet that they outpopulated the Humans, but only by a bit. Though none of them knew for certain, the current estimate was that they had about four hundred planets compared to the three hundred the Humans occupied. They'd also had many more systems of government that had all come together in the war effort.

But who were they fighting?

Jun called the meeting to order, as it were. She turned off the translator for a moment and spoke with Wyrak in his language.

Wyrak still complained sometimes about the accent she used, but did greet her back.

Then Jun turned the translator back on and dug out the tablet she'd brought over with her that day.

Rosey and Kalesen had already developed an adapter so that the Humans could connect their tablets to the Lithic ship and use their screens in the conference room.

Though Jun had invited Wyrak and the others over to *The Roadrunner* or *Aisha,* none of the Lithic were leaving their ship. Rosey still wasn't certain why.

She knew they were curious. Maybe they didn't feel safe, though. They didn't appear to have something of a stretchsuit, which the Humans always wore when visiting.

Jun connected her tablet, then displayed a picture of the Atoylee on the ship's screen.

Rosey had never paid that much attention to the aliens that Humanity had run across. She gazed just as curiously as Wyrak did at the four arms, the "petals" that surrounded the face of the alien, their tall, willowy stature.

Wyrak seemed fascinated.

"This is the second alien race that we've run across," Jun told Wyrak. "As you know, I'm a xenolinguist. I study alien languages."

Wyrak nodded, seemingly curious where this was going.

Rosey already knew, and swallowed against a dry throat.

"As I've said, the Atoylee and the Huzzomi were already dead by the time we discovered them," Jun said.

Then she brought up an image of the elevator room, on the base of Lawaka. Sano (or probably Dennis) had enhanced the colors, making them seem vibrant and alive.

"The Atoylee were a bit more advanced than the Huzzomi. Possibly quite a bit more, now that we've found a base that they'd set up on the moon," Jun continued. "We don't believe that they had discovered hyperspace. But they were able to build equipment that worked for centuries, deep underground, on this base."

Jun showed pictures of the staircase, the endless amount of stairs, leading to the base below. Again, someone had colored in part of the design, only this time, as Jun ran video, the images were side by side: on the left side was how the base appeared today, while the right side showed the geometric designs in their original beauty.

"We discovered many papers in this base, detailing the work that the Atoylee scientists had been doing," Jun continued, scans of the ancient, hieroglyphic writing filling the screen.

Rosey appreciated Jun filling in the blanks, but her palms were starting to sweat.

"The Atoylee built many things out of plants, and chemicals, not machinery," Jun continued. "They were masters as genetic manipulation. It's why so little is alive, left on the planet below. Everything burned when they were bombed."

Wyrak seemed sad at that, as if he, too, would have liked meeting these sunflower people.

"The reason they built this base was because of the dangerous nature of what they were building. It wasn't just a bomb, but a chemical bomb," Jun said.

Wyrak shot Jun a look at that.

Though Rosey wasn't an expert in the Lithic body language, she'd still be willing to bet that Wyrak had just grown wary. She, herself, hadn't tensed up completely. No, really.

"Seems that the Atoylee were being attacked by some alien species," Jun continued on with. "They were destroyed, though, before they could deliver their weapon."

Jun paused, turning her eyes away from the screen and staring directly at Wyrak.

"Tell me. Do you know anything about the Bukoykan?"

Wyrak stiffened. One of the guards spoke sharply into his wristcomm.

More guards immediately entered the conference room.

Rosey and Jamaal shared a look.

Seemed they'd been right.

These Bukoykan were still around.

And possibly trying to destroy the other aliens they'd met.

Rosey held her hands up in the air as formerly friendly Lithic soldiers turned deadly serious, weapons pointed at her and the rest of the Humans.

Hopefully, she and the others could find common ground with the Lithic.

Or they might all be wiped out.

READ MORE!

Be sure to pick up all the books in the Live Alien Contact series.

Alien Wreck
Alien Codex
Alien Encounter
Alien War

Available at the Knotted Road Shop and your favorite retailers!

https://www.knottedroadpress.com/collections/live-alien-contact

ABOUT THE AUTHOR

Leah R Cutter writes page-turning fiction in exotic locations, such as a magical New Orleans, the ancient Orient, Hungary, the Oregon coast, rural Kentucky, Seattle, Minneapolis, and many others.

She writes literary, fantasy, mystery, science fiction, and horror fiction. Her short fiction has been published in magazines like *Alfred Hitchcock's Mystery Magazine* and *Talebones*, anthologies like Fiction River, and on the web. Her long fiction has been published both by New York publishers as well as small presses.

Find Leah's books on Knotted Road Press at (www.KnottedRoadPress.com)

Follow her blog at www.LeahCutter.com.

Reviews

It's true. Reviews help me sell more books. If you've enjoyed this story, please consider leaving a review of it on your favorite site.

Come someplace new...

Do you enjoy exploring strange new worlds, new cultures, new people?

Journey into the various lands envisioned by Leah R Cutter.

Sign up for my newsletter and I'll start you on your travels with a free copy of my book, *The Island Sampler*.

I will never spam you or use your email for nefarious purposes.
You can also unsubscribe at any time.

http://www.LeahCutter.com/newsletter/

ABOUT KNOTTED ROAD PRESS

Knotted Road Press publishes dynamic fiction set in exotic locations. Our authors cover a wide range of genres including science fiction, fantasy, mystery, literary, and poetry. We also have unique non-fiction voices in genres such as autobiography, business, cookbooks, and how-tos. We offer both DRM-free ebooks and print books for a global readership.

Knotted Road Press
www.KnottedRoadPress.com

www.ingramcontent.com/pod-product-compliance
Lightning Source LLC
Chambersburg PA
CBHW071515100726
47908CB00004B/1178